Chrysoprase

The Chalcedony Chronicles

Book Two

B. KRISTIN McMICHAEL

For my husband and my kids. I love my family. They make life worthwhile.

CONTENTS

PROLOGUE

The goddess sat and watched the events unfold. She was eternal and older than time, yet she still did not know how things would turn out. Time was a fluid concept. She could see the future and the past, but everything changed whenever someone like Marcella Navina was born. Mari was special. With the ability to traverse time, Mari could change the fate she was dealt, but the goddess was not sure that she would. Would the world change this time? Could Mari save everyone? Would Mari's ending stay the same? Would she make the same choices? The goddess hoped not. She hoped this time would lead to a new future. Mankind was depending on Mari, and they didn't even know it.

The goddess had tended to humans as her own children. She had been around when they were created. She loved them and nurtured them. They were innocent. But before she knew what was going on, man changed. They not only enslaved the earth and animals around them, they enslaved each other. They began wars and killed each other. They lost their respect of nature and all that was granted to them. Not all men deserved the life they were dealt, and many still respected the world around them. The best way she knew how to help the innocent was to cast her body into hundreds of chalcedony—stones of all colors which each held a part of her. Her power would allow those who were selected to travel through time, to right a future that went astray. It was a good solution, and it worked well for a long time. People sought her help to find answers. They would return to their time with knowledge, and better the world around them. But that was until the hardened quartz stones began mysteriously disappearing. Soon, they'd be all gone, and there would be nothing more the goddess could do. Her own body disappeared with her powers, and she was now reduced to just a shell. She could do little but watch and pray for someone to save her humans before they destroyed the world that they depended on. Marcella was her last chance. The goddess knew the heart of the girl was pure and true. She would do what was right. At least the goddess hoped that she would.

Mari was in a cave praying to the goddess. She didn't know the goddess' name, yet she called for the old deity alongside the two men with her. Goddess had been called so many names in her life that she wasn't sure herself what her first name was. The goddess watched and waited. She couldn't step in and help them now. She had warned Mari there would be costs to changing the past. The goddess had to see to those consequences. Mari was going to have to fight for the future everyone wanted, but the goddess would be cheering for her, no matter what ordeals she would have to overcome. All hope lied in the girl praying for her. Mari was the last child of time.

CHAPTER 1

CHANGING HOME

I got up early, seeing that I couldn't sleep anyway. I was too anxious to hear my boyfriend Seth's voice. I needed to reassure myself that this was all real. We had just returned from traveling to the ancient past, where we had to escape people who were trying to kidnap *me*, of all people, and what better way to disappear than to head back to the future. Even with all my doubt, we made it. I was in the present, and at home in my own bed. It was only five in the morning, on November twenty-third, Thanksgiving Day. I hadn't missed a day on my journey to the past and back. It was still hard to believe it was true, but we actually made it.

On top of everything, we learned my mother was from the past as well. She was a princess, of all things. I couldn't wait to tell her what I knew and what I had seen and to ask her some questions. How did she come from the past? Who was my father? Why did she leave? My little trip back had revealed that my mother had given birth to, and raised me, here in the present, but Seth's father knew my mother in the past. She was a princess from the Middle East sent off to marry the Pharaoh. While she never talked of her childhood, I could never have imagined that. She had a lot of explaining to do.

I looked at the clock and knew that even at this time my mother would be up baking. It was Thanksgiving Day, and there was always much to be done. I didn't have to join her until six, but she started earlier. It was our Thanksgiving tradition after all: the whole family dinner with a turkey, stuffing, mashed potatoes, and cranberries. The complete fixings everyone has, all made by my mother. My mother, the woman from the past who came to the future to raise me. My mother, who didn't have electricity where she had come from, yet could cook a turkey in our electric oven perfectly. My mother, a princess. That would certainly take some getting used to.

With everything changing so fast, I was grateful to be home. Seth was right; as long as we were together, we could do anything. We had found a way in his time to be together, and nothing would stop us now that we were in my time. I don't doubt the goddess had us meet for one reason—to fall in love. Seth was my other half. Being with him just felt right. I loved him. I regretted not having the chance to tell him that. Now I had to wait until after Thanksgiving to see him, and tell him that I loved him, too, since he returned to his home, and I returned to mine. I didn't even have a way to contact him until I was back at college.

I dressed quickly, choosing the longest sleeved shirt I could find to cover my arms. When I met the goddess to travel back to find Seth, she had marked my arm with the blessed carnelian stone that hung above my grandfather's desk. Now I had permanent lines on my left arm, and my grandfather was missing a rare artifact. After talking with Mom, I was going to have to apologize to Grandpa for losing his ancient carnelian necklace. Well, not so much lost, but reformed, into the light brown bands circling my left hand. I wasn't exactly sure how I was going to pass that one off yet. I needed to get back to college. I was sure Sim, my roommate and expert at keeping things covert from the parents, would be able to give me some good story to use. Right now I was flying solo on the story part, and I didn't know what I'd say. It was best to just cover it up for now.

I paused on my way out of my room and looked at the bright green stone lying on my dresser. It was another piece blessed by the goddess. I wasn't sure how many existed, but now I had two. Seth's friend Dee had given it to me to get me home when he didn't know about the carnelian I'd have forever in my arm. While made up of the same mineral—chalcedony—the apple green stone was different than the carnelian Seth had. Instead of a round stone, it was more angular, almost triangular. It was flatter and cooler to the touch. If Dee hadn't given it to me, I don't even know if I would have looked closer at it. I had looked up all the chalcedony types before my search, for one to go into the past, but I didn't remember the distinct green stone I had now. I dropped it back onto my dresser and left my room.

I descended the stairs soundlessly and stopped in the darkened kitchen. I had checked my clock enough times to know I had the day right. Something was really off. It was quiet, too quiet for it being Thanksgiving. The counters were bare, and not a dish was being prepared. It wasn't like my mother just left for a moment--it was like she had never started. Panic was starting to set in. I looked around the kitchen and nothing was there. It was empty. There were no pies being mixed, and no turkey thawing in the sink. What was going on?

Worrying that I had the date wrong, even though I knew I didn't, I ran down the hallway to my grandfather's study. He was always up before my mom was, and a light was on and shining under through the cracks. I knocked and pushed the door open before there could be any response. I stopped in the doorway and just stared into the room. Inside my grandfather was sleeping on his couch

5

while someone else sat at his desk. Mr. Sangre stood as I walked in.

"Hello, Marcella," Mr. Sangre said. I stared at him, unable to respond. Why was the time gatekeeper, and adoptive father to my boyfriend, in my house, and why was he with my grandfather? "Your grandfather just fell asleep. Can we go somewhere where we can talk and not disturb him?"

I nodded and numbly led him back out of the room and into the kitchen. My stomach sank. Something had to be wrong if Mr. Sangre, the time-travelling gatekeeper, who ushered people between times, was in my house. This was the same Mr. Sangre I had met three weeks earlier to tell me that Seth had gone home. He had not yet been a bearer of good news for me. We stopped in the empty kitchen. It hurt to look around and not find my mother cooking. I already guessed that something happened, but the sudden appearance of Mr. Sangre made me dread what I feared was the reason.

"Your mother's time here was up last night. She was sent home just after midnight, four hours ago. The goddess felt it would be too much to remove all the memories your grandfather had with her in them. I was beside him when it happened. He fell asleep after spending four hours going over everything with me. I told him the truth, and he is grasping as much of it as he can," Mr. Sangre told me. This was what I dreaded. There was one rule about time travel. The time you're from is the time you must die in. Everyone had to return to their time at some point.

I stared at him and tried to process what he was saying. My mother disappeared hours ago. She just vanished and was gone. Because she wasn't of my time, for everyone else, she never existed. No one I knew would even remember her. I sat down in the chair next to me before my legs failed to keep me standing. In this time period, I was now technically an orphan with no father or mother. The shock hit me hard, but no tears came. It didn't feel real. It couldn't be real. My mother was gone. That didn't even sound real. When I finally looked up, Mr. Sangre was waiting for me to say something.

"Four hours," I repeated. Mr. Sangre nodded. I had just returned four hours ago.

Had this been the goddess' plan all along? She had warned me my travels through time would affect everything, but I thought she was meaning on a larger scale. If I started a war, then that would change history, and the future. I hadn't thought that my travels would mean my mother would have to go back. I didn't do anything associated with her. There was no reason to send Mom back. She had nothing left there. She ran away from that life and spent the last nineteen years here. She had lived more of her life in the present than in the past. My mother belonged here with me and my grandfather. My heart was breaking. What would my grandfather do without her? We were his only family. It was just him and me now, and I wasn't even sure I'd end up staying in this time, either. Would he be left all alone some day? I couldn't do that to him. My mother wouldn't do that to him.

"I told your grandfather I'd stay until he woke," Mr. Sangre said, still watching me for the breakdown that was bound to come as soon as I could actually get some tears out. "I should go back to watch over him. You can imagine it was quite a shock, and it will take time to process it all."

I nodded and watched him walk away. The latch on grandfather's study door clicked shut, and I was alone. I really needed to get back to college and find Seth. Right about now I needed a hug. Time was moving, and everything around me was changing too fast. I wanted it to slow down. I wanted life to go back to normal. I wanted to keep Seth and my mother both. Why did it feel like I was choosing between them? Why did either of them have to leave? Why couldn't they just stay in the present with me? Why did it have to be so complicated?

I didn't even notice the time pass as I stared off out the window to our backyard. There was frost on the ground, but no snow like college. I thought of the snow at college, the light, fluffy stuff falling from the sky carefree. It was a distraction, but only for a moment. Then I was back to my current dilemma. How could my mother be gone? It didn't seem fair. She belonged here in this time with me and my grandfather. It just couldn't be possible that she was a princess from another time. It was just too unreal.

When I finally got up from the kitchen stool, I went back to my room and noticed a letter on my desk. I had looked at my dresser as I left and the green stone that was sitting there, but I hadn't looked at my desk. I sat down on my bed and opened it.

Dearest Child,

My time here is ending. I have known since you went off to college that my time would end soon. The goddess had promised me to let me stay here until you grew up. I knew that day would come, but I have been dreading telling you about my past. First, I didn't think you would believe me, and then I didn't want to tell you as I was ashamed. The goddess reassured me you would understand, so this is what you need to know.

I grew up as a princess in a time in the past. I don't even know where or when I was born, just that my life was one of privilege. As privileged as I was to always have food and a roof over my head, I also had no say in my future. When I turned sixteen, I was given to a man twice my age in a political marriage. My marriage would secure trade routes for both sides. I didn't know the man. I didn't love him. It didn't matter. Before I could ever even meet him, someone tried to kill me. I don't know if it was from within the palace, or someone outside the palace. All I know is there was another man that had saved me. He protected me from the attack, and stayed beside me as I healed.

When I recovered, I was sent across the desert to the king I was promised to. By this time, I found out what love was. I loved the man who saved me, and I was pregnant with his child. We didn't know what to do. We could run away and start over, but it was not that easy back then. The man I loved was a military man. All he had ever known was the military. He had no trade, and I was a princess. I could sing and play board games, but knew nothing of tending a house or cooking a meal. Neither of us were suited to start over. The worst part was that if anyone found out about you, the man would have been killed. Agreeing to the engagement made me the property of the king I was to marry. My love had touched the king's property. No one could save him, not even his best friend, the young general that ran the military. Paramessu had his own young son to protect; he could not protect his friend or me.

When my love heard there was a way to get away from all of it, we found a site dedicated to the goddess. We prayed together, and she answered by sending me here. My love was left there alone, knowing that we would be protected. When your grandfather found me hidden in his *artifacts during a trip overseas, he brought me back, and he lied to get me into the country by claiming me as his child. I had you seven months later, and the rest you know.*

I never meant for this to stay a secret for so long. You would need to know some day, but I was too ashamed. Rather than stay and try to live out a new life with the man I loved, your father, I chose the easy way- to run. I have never regretted the decision to keep you safe, but I regret that you never knew your father. I wish you had known him, and he you. He was a great man, destined for great things. I know everything worked for the best, but I can't change the past.

I just hope I taught you enough. I know you are a wonderful young lady. I wish I could be around to see you grow up and get married. I wish I would see my grandchildren. I wish I could stay with you forever, but I can't. I'm not of your time, and never will be. I have to accept that, and hope that I taught you enough. Never think that I didn't love you. Never think that your father didn't love you. And when you find that one man that steals your heart someday, don't let him get away. Love is worth fighting for.

-Mom

I stared hard at the letter and read it over two more times. I had tried to convince myself that it was all a dream and not real, but deep down I knew it was true. She was from the past. Seth's father, the general, was right. My mom was a princess. Now, after reading my mother's words, I couldn't deny it any longer. My life just got a lot more complicated, and a lot emptier. I felt bad for my mother then and now. I couldn't even begin to imagine her life, being sent off to marry a man she didn't know. I really needed to talk to Seth.

Everything was crashing down around me. Nothing seemed real to me now. My mother was gone. I could travel into the past and future. People here might not actually be from here, and there was no one that would remember my mother beyond my grandfather and me. She would just disappear like Seth did.

It wasn't fair. The goddess let me meet Seth, and let me go back and get him, but now it seemed like she was making me choose between them. By going to the past to get Seth back I had lost my mother. Would it be the same in reverse now if I went back to get my mother? Would the goddess take Seth? I know neither of them was from my time, but it still wasn't fair. Why couldn't they stay here? Seth was here for three years. My mother was here for over nineteen. There was no reason to send her back right at the moment the goddess did. Why couldn't I have a little bit of time with both my mother and Seth here?

I stood and paced my room. This wasn't right. The goddess may have good intentions for bringing people together, and maybe she was the reason I was alive at all since my mother and I could have been put to death for her falling in love with my father. I have no clue what happened to the babies of women who were disloyal to their king, but I still felt robbed. I never knew my father, and my mother was now lost to the past. There had to be a solution. I looked up on the dresser as I passed it. The shiny green stone stared back. Was that stone the key? Could I go back and bring my mother back also?

A plan was forming in my head. If I could find out how to get to my mother, could I take her back to the future with me? I had no clue how the time travel thing worked. The last time was more of a fluke than anything. I was just following the thread that bound me to Seth. I didn't have the same connection with my mother, but there had to be a way. I wasn't going to give up on her. She traveled to an unknown world to protect me, I would do the same for her.

I walked back over to the new stone in my collection. I rubbed the smooth green rock in my hand as I debated in my head. There had to be a way to get to my mother and save her from the past.

I had two options. First, I could go and ask the man down the hallway how to travel in time. Mr. Sangre was a time gatekeeper after all, but I doubted he would tell me any more than he already had. I'd asked him before how to find Seth, and he didn't really tell me how to do it. The second option was to ask the goddess, but I was unsure if that was a good idea either. She had just ripped my mother out of my life, and I wasn't exactly sure I could be civil to her at this point. If she asked me why I wanted to learn, I'd have to lie to her so that she wouldn't try to stop me.

"I see the dilemma," a deep female voice said from somewhere in my room. I could not see her, but I knew that it was the goddess.

"You should see it. You created it," I replied. I had to bite my tongue from saying more. She had taken my mother from me.

"I have taken nothing from you," the goddess answered. She didn't seem at all worried about my growing anger.

"You took her back. There was no reason to take her back right now," I replied to the empty room. It was easier to not have the goddess there physically. I had the feeling she knew that, too.

"I told you that you cannot change the past without changing the future," the goddess answered. There was no anger to her voice, or even judgment. She simply stated the fact.

"But I thought you meant big events," I answered, sitting down and finally halting my pacing around the room. The new green stone was still between my fingers.

"My deal with your mother was to allow her to stay here as long as you were growing up," the goddess answered. I still could not see her, but got the feeling she was right beside me now. "In my mind, growing up was always going to be the time that you figured out how to time travel."

"But I'm not grown up. I don't really know how to time travel, and I still need my mother," I complained, trying to keep tears at bay. Yes, going off to college, living on my own, having a new exciting life made me feel grown up a bit, but I wasn't there yet. I still needed my mother.

I felt a breeze caress my back in the windless room. I knew it was the goddess and would have been upset by the comfort she tried to offer, but now my anger was gone and replaced by sadness.

"Mari, you are strong. Life will never be easy for you with the gift you have. No one else remembers it all like you will. You will find no one like you, but know that I believe in you," the goddess said cryptically.

"Strong or not, I need her back," I answered stubbornly.

"But this isn't her time," the goddess replied. That was true, but it still didn't make it right.

"What makes it not her time?" I asked. "She spent more time here than in the past. The life she knew was here. How can this not be her time?" I tried to logically fight with the goddess. I did have a valid point.

"I didn't make the rules, and I cannot change them. One must return to where they are born," the goddess replied. Her voice was farther away now. She sounded as if she we standing on the other side of the room. "But not all is lost. Mari, you can see your mom any time you wish. That is why I made sure to wait to take her from you. You now have the power to travel to her. I cannot change the past, or her fate, but I made sure you would never have to stay apart from her."

"But how?" I asked desperately.

"You'll learn in time. This cannot be rushed. You will learn," the goddess' replied as her voice began to fade. I felt that her presence was gone from the room. I was alone again.

The goddess's words were comforting, but it wasn't enough. I sat back down on my bed and looked closer at the green stone. The etchings on the back were illegible, as they had been before, but I knew the secret to that now. I wanted to add a drop of blood and see if it would work, but I had to stop myself. I couldn't run off quite yet. I needed to make a plan. There was no way I could leave her in that time, forced to marry someone she wasn't in love with. No matter what the goddess said, my mother needed me, and she needed me to save her. I was going to get my mother back, but I'd need some help. I needed someone with a good grasp of what I was walking into. I wasn't going to be unprepared this time. There was one person I could count on.

I got up and ran back to my grandfather's study. I needed to talk to Seth right away. He was up in the Twin Cities with his adoptive family, and he didn't have a cell phone. Only he could use the excuse that he was too old for a cell phone. But I knew that it wouldn't matter. There was one way to talk to Seth. He was Mr. Sangre's adopted child, after all, and Mr. Sangre happened to be sitting in my house.

Grandfather was still asleep as I entered, and I moved closer to Mr. Sangre while trying not to wake my grandfather. It was hard to look at my grandfather. He looked like he had aged ten years overnight. The strain of losing my mother was tough on him. Mr. Sangre looked up from his book as I came closer.

"Do you have a phone number that I can reach Seth at?" I asked. Since we had returned to when we had left, Mr. Sangre should have already met the boys on their return weeks ago. Seth didn't have a cell phone, but I doubted that he lived in a house without a landline phone in it.

Mr. Sangre looked startled by the question.

"I can give you the number to call Ty. He stayed back at their house on the lake for the holiday," Mr. Sangre said.

I looked at him. That was weird. Why would I call Ty instead of Seth?

"But I'm sorry to be the one to tell you this, Mari. You won't be able to reach Seth by phone. He didn't come back with Ty."

My world crashed down. I didn't just lose my mother in my trip to the past; I had lost my boyfriend, too.

CHAPTER 2

PIECES OF MY PAST

I looked at the clock. It was already eight p.m. Sometime during my crying I had fallen asleep. I glanced at my phone. It was ringing again. That must have been why I woke up. I didn't rush to answer it, since it wouldn't be who I wanted to hear from anyways. A ringing phone made no difference now since Seth wasn't here in my time. Who else would be calling me? It didn't matter. Unless it was Ty calling. No one else would remember Seth, and I didn't want to deal with that again. My heart broke the last time they were all forgotten; I didn't think I could handle it again. I should talk to Ty and see what was going on, but I just wasn't ready. I didn't take the number from Mr. Sangre. Instead, he'd left it on my desk next to my phone at some point.

Tears built behind my eyes as I thought about everything. Sleep had been easier. I didn't think when I was sleeping. The world I didn't want to deal with could just fade away. How could the goddess take both Seth and my mother? It wasn't fair. She didn't even let me have one of them. How was I supposed to go on without both of them in my life?

The phone kept ringing, and I was tempted to not even pick it up. But it could be Ty. Maybe Ty would have answers about how to help me. I really needed a friend right about now. Ty could help, maybe.

I picked up my phone and didn't even look to see who was calling. I was on autopilot as I just pushed the on button.

"Hello," I answered.

"Mari," my best friend from high school, Amy, squealed into the phone. "I have been calling you for days." She was practically shouting now. "I'm so in need of seeing you."

"Hi, Amy," I replied, trying to fake some cheerfulness.

"Just hi?" Amy responded. "Not even a 'how're you doing?' Or 'how many hot guys have you dated in the past two months while we were forced to live states away from each other?'"

I had to smile a little. It was Amy, after all. There was no getting her down. She saw the rainbow behind every storm. Her cheerfulness was always contagious, even when I was sad.

"Hi, Amy. What's your 'hot guy' record up to now?" I replied, knowing that was exactly what she wanted to talk about.

"I found three new ones in the first week. You really should have stayed here in Chicago with me. I was missing my partner. I mean, *come on!* It was *you* that the guys were chasing after. Your red hair always made you stand out. You would have pulled in twice as many, and then I'd have had so many more to pick from," Amy babbled on. "What was so important in that frozen state that you could only text me and never call me back? I missed you, chicka."

"I missed you, too," I replied. I cringed a little. I had been a bit neglectful of my Chicago friends.

In truth, I *had* missed her. We'd been inseparable in

high school. But once I went off to college in Minnesota, things were just different. I couldn't relate to the life Amy was living back here in Chicago. She was going to clubs, and hitting the same old places we hung out in while we were in high school. I doubt she even made any new close friends. She was a big city girl in every way possible, and I was in a small town that was lucky to have two fast food joints in it. I knew what she would say if I called. It was what she told me every week of the summer before I left. Why the heck did I want to go off to some little liberal arts college in the middle of nowhere? What was wrong with me?

"Well that's great. Then you'll be up for going over to the Jones place later," Amy babbled on.

"Um, I'm not really up to going out tonight," I replied. And I wasn't ever going to be up for going to my high school ex-boyfriend's house.

"That is exactly what I knew you would say. That's why I already talked to your grandfather, and he said it would be good for you," Amy answered. "He said you needed to get out and blow off some steam. He agreed that a party would be a good idea."

"What?" My grandfather hated how all the teenagers partied.

"You've avoided me since you moved off to the middle of nowhere. You owe me. I got the whole *I have to spread my wings and fly* thing, but really... Minnesota? Why so far away? It's almost like you were trying to get away from us." I could almost hear Amy pouting through the phone, like I personally insulted her by moving away. "Are you ready to come back here now? I bet you miss it. The Chicago life. Or any city life for that matter. How could you not?"

"I'm not moving back," I replied. We had been arguing about this for over a month before we just stopped talking. She was convinced that I had enough time away, and needed to come back.

"Sure you're not," Amy teased. My friends really thought I'd move back after a semester. Actually, most of them gave me two weeks before I'd miss home. It didn't happen. "Then I'll pick you up in ten minutes for the party?"

"Ten minutes?" I asked. She lived farther than ten minutes away.

"Ten minutes," Amy responded before hanging up without waiting for me to protest.

I sat up and pulled my fingers through my hair. There was no way I wanted to go off to a house party, but I was sure Amy wasn't going to take no for an answer. I had no chance to talk her out of it. If I had just not answered my phone, I could have avoided all this. I looked down at my shirt and jeans. I was wrinkled, but didn't care. I didn't need to impress anyone at the party. After going off to college, and seeing something outside the little circle I grew up in, I was sure I didn't have any plans to come back. No one at this party would even understand that. We'd grown up in Chicago, living our lives all around each other. No one else wanted to even venture to another suburb. Everyone just wanted to continue living on their parents' wealth and having fun.

My hair was combed enough with my fingers, and I grabbed a sweatshirt. As I pulled it over my head, I heard a knock. That was faster than ten minutes. She was probably sitting in my driveway the whole time.

"Coming," I shouted at the door.

The door opened, and my grandfather stepped into the room. He had changed his clothes since I saw him sleeping this morning, but he still looked different. The bounce in his step was less evident, and his smile didn't reach his eyes. Sudden loss was hard for anyone to take. He was dealing with the same pain as I was, and I was sure I looked the same.

"Hey, sweetie," he said quietly.

"Hi, Grandpa," I replied, unsure what to say to him. I sat back down on my bed.

"Amy should be here soon. I wanted to be sure you were awake when she arrived," he said, explaining why he was up in my room. He rarely came up here, said it was too girly for him, but he was just giving me space. He was pretty cool like that.

"I got her call," I replied. "But I don't exactly want to go."

My grandfather smiled and laughed. "I figured as much. You are so like your mother. If I let you, I bet you would hibernate all day in your room. No, even more than all day. I bet you'd hibernate all Thanksgiving weekend in your room."

I shrugged. That was the plan. I didn't need to leave my room for anything but food.

"You can't do that, Mari. You can't let your life halt because your mother disappeared from it. I'm grateful James was here and let me keep my memories of your mother. I can only imagine how hard this must be for you, too. It feels like she should be here, but she isn't and we can't change that. I'd never change the fact that she came from the past in the first place. Your mother made my life worthwhile." He stopped by my dresser and picked up the green stone Dee had given me.

"Taking an interest in chalcedony now?" He turned the stone over in his hand. "Like my missing carnelian?"

I wanted to smack my head. Yep, he would have noticed that. Even in his grief my grandfather noticed that his framed carnelian necklace was gone. I hadn't even had time to come up with an excuse. I pulled up my sleeve to show him the reddish-brown lines. They were faded now, or maybe it was the lighting.

"Well, I planned to put it back after I used it, but it kind of got smashed into my arm permanently," I replied sheepishly.

My grandfather set the green stone down with a stern look on his face. "We've talked about taking items from the house without permission."

I knew exactly what he was talking about. I had only gone into his office once to snoop when I was eight. All the old stuff was enticing to me back then. I wanted to touch it all, and that wasn't the best thing—handling all the old artifacts. I got caught and was punished badly enough that I never once even went back into that room without knocking first. I learned my lesson well that day.

"I swear I was just going to borrow it," I added. I wasn't planning to keep it.

He smiled then, and laughed at me for my response.

"James explained it to me. He told me that the carnelian was actually from the goddess, and that it was always meant for you. I was just teasing you." My grandfather laughed. It was more hollow sounding than normal, but it got him to smile a little. "It must have been the reason you were in there years ago. It probably called to you. What is this one? It looks like chrysoprase."

"I have no idea what it is. It was given to me by Seth's friend. I think it's also from the goddess." I shrugged. It was strange to talk to my grandfather about it, but he was part of this new weird world now.

Grandfather rubbed the stone and stared hard at it, like it held the clue to where my mother was. I stood up and hugged him. He would always miss her as much as I did. He never married or had kids, but he never felt the need to with me and my mother in his life. Even with me going off to college, he always had my mother around. Now his great big house would be empty when I went back to college. He would be all alone.

"I will find her and bring her back," I told him as he placed his arms around me.

"I never doubted that," he said into the top of my head.

21

"But for now, be a kid and live a little. Go out with Amy. She's been really worried about you. I think she's stopped by over half a dozen times 'on accident' in the past few months, looking for you."

He patted my back before letting me go. He went to the door and smiled at me with his sad new smile. After one last look from the doorway he was gone, shuffling down the hallway.

The party was in full swing by the time we got there. That was typical Amy. She liked to arrive late. She felt that it made her presence even more important. It was still strange to find that nothing had changed. I thought it just made us late. I was used to it by now. It never used to bother me, but now it did. Amy was still Amy, but I felt like I was a completely new person.

"Did you hear that Logan still hasn't gotten a new girlfriend after you dumped him last year?" Amy grabbed my arm and pulled me into the house when I hesitated at the door. This was the house of my ex-boyfriend after all.

I shook my head. I hadn't heard that, but it didn't matter. I wasn't connected to the gossip circle like her. I didn't care who Logan was dating or cheating on now. He wasn't my concern. Good luck to whomever he suckered into dating him. They could have the fun time of him running off at any day or time. I didn't ever want to be back in his presence, but I couldn't turn Amy down. She wasn't one for taking no for an answer. Ever observant, Amy noticed my indifference.

"You did find someone at college," Amy intuitively guessed. I didn't want to reply or deny it. I couldn't lie to her. She was my oldest friend. "Once you say hi to everyone, I'm going to have to get you cornered alone to hear all the details. You can't date someone new without giving me a chance to assess him. You better show me a picture, and the more skin the better."

Amy waved to another one of our friends as we walked down the lavish hallway. I noticed her, but was busy looking around. I was always impressed by the Jones house. In my two years dating Logan, I had been over often. Everything was decorated in a very regal manner, and when most homes had a new/old look to them where the homeowner tried to fake authenticity, the Jones home was *old* old. Everything from the floors to the ceiling was vintage and authentic. I first didn't notice it, but my grandfather told me that everything in the house was real, and really old. The antiques around the entry room alone would cost a fortune.

Logan Jones came from money. I had no clue what his parents did, and in the two years I dated him, I never met his parents. They were always gone on business, but it must have been good business to afford him everything even most adults wanted. Without parents around in the gigantic house, you'd think he'd be alone, but that wasn't the case either. There were butlers, maids, cooks, and people to do just about anything for him. He could have whatever he wanted, and could do basically anything he wanted. It was amazing what money could buy you. My grandfather had money, but nothing like Logan. I always felt like a commoner around him.

"Amy, Mari," Stephanie Miller called out to the both of us.

Steph ran down the hallway, sliding the last few feet in her socks on the polished floor. We stopped her slide as she threw her arms around us in a big hug.

"You found our missing sister!" Steph cheered, hanging on tight.

In high school we were the three musketeers. We did everything together. I don't even think I took more than half a dozen classes that didn't have either Steph or Amy in them. They were my everything. I hugged Steph back. How could she be familiar, yet so different now? The people were the same, and just as I remembered them, but something felt different.

Steph looped her arms through mine and Amy's, pulling us back to the party room. I had no choice but to reluctantly go with them. In reality, I'd have been happy to sit in the car. It was too weird to be back with everyone. Nothing had changed, and I really didn't want to see Logan or his friends. This wasn't my world any more. But Amy would never let me sit out there alone. She was determined to make me have a good time.

"When did you get home?" Steph asked.

I didn't answer as I looked around the house. There was something magical about this place. I always thought that. Too bad it had to be Logan Jones' house. Amy and Steph stopped, so I stopped along with them. Then I realized Steph was talking to me. Guess it had to be me as I remembered the question. Amy really hadn't gone anywhere to get home from.

"A few days ago," I replied. By this time I wasn't completely sure. My memory of the past three months was a bit hazy with the change in time without Seth in it. My memories were all a bit mushed together right now.

"And it took you a few days to call us?" Steph asked accusingly.

It was true. The old me from high school would have called them before I made it into the driveway, but the new me was a bit more preoccupied. I shrugged to her as my response. There wasn't anything I could actually say that wouldn't make it seem like something was up, or like I completely ditched them.

"She's got a boyfriend," Amy replied in hushed tones as we neared the noise of the party in progress.

"A boyfriend?" Steph squealed. "I need to see." She

grabbed my phone before I could stop her. I normally would have protested, but she would find nothing there. Amy grabbed my phone back and gave it to me before Steph could look through it.

"Later," she promised over the noise. Steph led us into the room filled with both students from my old high school, St. Maria's Preparatory, and Bishop Glenwood, the male school we did everything with.

Steph wove between the groups of people standing around. I recognized most of them, but was glad we didn't stop to say hi. I felt disconnected from everyone. What would I say to them? Could I continue to smile and take the ribbing about Minnesota? I actually liked it there. Steph wove her way further into the room and a couch that was miraculously empty. She pulled us down to sit before anyone else could, and was right back to talking with Amy about the latest gossip she had heard.

I ended up pretending that I cared about their conversation, too. I was really too removed to even know what they were complaining about now. Someone named Ned got in a fight with someone else named Jim at some club because they were from different colleges. I didn't really get it. So I looked around the room instead. There were many people I hadn't seen in months, yet I recognized most. People were still staggered around the room where you would expect them. Most people hung out with the same groups. Group A was glaring at Group B, while Group C was checking out Group D. Nothing was any different than when we were in high school. I looked down at the clothes Amy insisted I wear as my usual jeans and sweatshirt were not 'Amy party approved.' I was wearing the same kind of clothes I did in high school, and I was sitting with my same two best friends. From the outside, nothing had changed here either.

Unfortunately, from our seat, and in my distraction of looking around the room, I found Logan Jones. He was one person I never wanted to see again. We didn't exactly have a nice break up. In fact, I had yet to talk to him since the day I said I was finished with him.

Logan was at the pool table with Becca Chance. I had known Becca since we were in grade school. She was the princess type that did whatever she wanted and got whatever she wanted from Daddy. He would move the world if she asked. She wasn't accustomed to being told no. I had no doubt that she had been aggressively pursuing Logan since before we broke up. Becca was needy and demanding, which made such a nice combination. I almost felt sorry for him. *Almost.*

Becca was leaning down to the table to hit a ball, obviously doing her best to show off her only asset—ones Daddy bought for her sixteenth birthday.

"And did you hear about Sara and Sam?" Steph asked me, trying to get me to join the conversation going on beside me. I shook my head *no*. I really hadn't heard about anyone, and didn't really care. I wasn't into the high school gossip circle anymore.

"How could you not hear about them?" Amy replied, surprised.

"Umm, you know, eight hours away in the cold snow. She walks up hill both ways to get to class," Steph teased.

I smiled along with them as they laughed, but it still stung. I remember how much they teased me before I had left. I joked right along with them. I was too scared to be able to tell them I was really excited to go so far away. They wouldn't have understood. I really felt like I was moving off to the middle of nowhere, and I was scared completely. It would have been nice to have them support me and tell me that I would do great. It wasn't the same now. I had lived there for three and a half months. It was more like home than this place was. I didn't need their support. I actually did do just fine moving away. That one little step made me feel like I could do anything.

"I'm kind of busy with classes," I replied, answering Amy's question about hearing gossip before they could continue teasing me.

"Or with boys." Amy winked at me. That part was very much true. Seth had spent all semester, thus far, trying to get me to go out with him. A large part of my extra time did have to do with boys, or one boy in particular.

Amy still didn't get her chance to corner me alone, and she knew I wasn't going to say anything with everyone sitting around us. I mean, my ex-boyfriend was only feet away, and he wouldn't like to hear about my new dates. I wasn't looking forward to that grilling. What was I going to tell her? My imaginary boyfriend, who doesn't exist in our time, but who I plan to bring back, went to my school before he disappeared. That would be believable. Luckily for me, someone shouted from the wet bar, and I was saved from talking further.

"Come and get it," some guy from Bishop Glenwood shouted a second time.

I followed Amy and Steph as they stood and joined everyone heading over to the bar and the games that were sure to follow. I took a glass of whatever Amy shoved into my hand. I looked down at the drink and didn't even have to consider drinking it. Normally I was all for fun with my friends, but now I wasn't sure I should ever have a drink. What would happen if I got drunk? Could I end up time traveling somewhere I didn't know? Could I get stuck in the past, or maybe the future? It was scary enough to chase after Seth into the unknown when I was going straight to him, but now it was even scarier, thinking that I could end up anywhere in any time.

Fortunately, Amy and Steph didn't see my hesitation as we made it back to some empty seats. This time it wasn't with a view of the pool table in case Logan and Becca were still there. I still didn't have feelings for Logan, and really my opinion of him wasn't that high, but even he didn't deserve to end up with Becca. She had been chasing Logan since before I met him my sophomore year, and even us being together didn't stop her. He had made it very clear to me that he didn't appreciate anything about Becca, but now he seemed to not mind. That was guys for you.

Amy and Steph took a few sips, and I pretended to as well. There was no way I could tell them about my new lack of interest in drinking. It would be one more thing for them to tease me about in regards to Morton. It wasn't even college that did it to me, but they would blame it on my school again. And I surely couldn't tell them the truth. They would send me to a shrink; probably someone's father right here in the room, or it was likely that someone here had one on speed dial.

It didn't take long before the party was in full swing. Amy's words were a bit slurred as she and Steph stood to go join the game of beer pong. Amy was always a lightweight. She kind of reminded me of Sim. I missed my roomie a bit more now. At least she wouldn't take every opportunity to throw in a jab about Morton like my two friends had all evening.

"I'm going to go to the bathroom," I told Steph, the more sober of the two. I was planning to walk by the bathroom at least, so I technically wasn't lying to my half-sober friend. Not that it would matter anyway.

"We can come with," Steph offered, spilling her latest filled drink a little.

"Nah, I'll be right back," I replied, and hurried away from them before either could follow.

It took a little maneuvering to make it out of the party without anyone stopping me, but soon I was in the quieter hallway. People were still coming and going, but no one would pay attention to me turning further into the house. Mostly everyone had a little, if not a lot, to drink by now. The Jones house was huge, but at least I knew my way around. I figured I had at least an hour or two to waste before Amy would be too drunk to protest us leaving early. That much hadn't seemed to change. Lucky for me Amy was still Amy.

I wandered down the hallway to the library. No one from the party was bound to walk this way. I could wait until everyone was really drunk before I returned, and no one would notice that I hadn't been drinking while I was whisking Amy away. I opened the door slowly. Just because I didn't see anyone else in the house, that didn't mean they weren't there. The Jones family had people working everywhere in the house. I poked my head in and smiled. The library was lit dimly, but no one was inside. It was quiet and empty, just how I wanted to find it.

I closed the door behind me and let the silence settle. I've always liked libraries, and the Jones library was no exception. It was as beautiful as the rest of the house, with books that lined the walls two stories high in beautiful wooden bookcases that were always polished, though I rarely found anyone working in the room in the two years I dated Logan. The books were not modern books, and I had yet to find something published in the last three or four decades. It was a magical room, just like the rest of the house. Everything in the room was ancient. The books were of dark hues of red, blue, and green with ornate gold and silver writing on the spines that lined the walls from floor to ceiling. The antique ladders that dotted the walls let you get the upper books, but I never went up that far. It was enough for me to peruse the selections at ground level.

As I strolled back further I looked at what was in the reading boxes. Some of the books were so old they were kept in clear display boxes. They were the books that had to be handled with the utmost care, and those the Jones deemed truly display worthy. I peered into the closest box and looked at the ancient writing. The gold strokes had always been illegible to me, but fun to look at none-the-less. These old pages made history real for me before I had the ability to travel through time. Someone hundreds of years ago had sat somewhere by candlelight, writing the pages I glanced at. They had spent long hours making what would last through the ages. It truly made you appreciate time, not that that was an issue now. My new ability to travel through time made me understand that even better. But there was still something to be said about these old texts.

I looked up. It felt like someone was watching me. I glanced around the room. The door was still closed, and no one was around. I hadn't heard anyone enter. Their maids were silent, but not that silent. I looked back around the room. The feeling was still there, but I was alone.

My focus went back to the documents scattered around the room in glass cases. One toward the far window caught my attention. The carnelian lines around my hand pulsated as if to tell me I was going in the right direction. The tingles in my arm felt much like they did when I was around Seth. I missed him so much, and I was nowhere near knowing how to get him back. It was like Seth was sending me a sign even though we were far apart. I moved slowly down the line of books. Something was calling to the stone that was now imprinted into my arm. I stopped at each book as I passed. Why was one calling to me and all the others not? As I got close to the one I really wanted to see, I paused again. I still felt like someone was watching me. I looked down at the words on the page in the box in front of me. They weren't the ones calling to me, yet were pretty all the same.

"Figured this would be where you ran off to," Logan said quietly from somewhere in the room.

I was sure I didn't hear him enter, and I had no clue how long he had been there. He stepped out of the shadow he was hidden in and slowly slunk across the room. Logan had always puzzled me. Around everyone else, you would think he was just another very friendly jock, but alone, he was completely different. His movements were always perfect and graceful, but he kept that hidden from everyone else. I remember the first time I was alone with him. Logan was exciting, and he made me feel like I was the one he had spent his life hunting. I still felt that vibe from him, but now it was just confusing. I didn't have feelings for him anymore, beyond the annoyance I still felt about our last date. That would probably last forever. The reason I didn't trust guys in general, and rightfully so, was standing in front of me now. Having him slowly analyzing me was strange. I still got butterflies in my stomach—anyone would get that when someone as hot as him was looking at you. But I didn't have the loving feelings that once went with those butterflies.

I didn't answer, but kept slowly walking, glancing down at each box I passed. As I neared the one I really wanted to see, I only glanced down at it like I had the others. I didn't need Logan wanting to know more than I could possibly explain, nor did I especially want to talk to him about anything at this point. The box still called to me, and I wanted to stare at it more. The writing, while illegible to me, looked familiar. It almost felt like if I reached in and touched the old paper I would see what it had to say. I clasped my hands behind my back and kept walking. Logan followed behind. I finally stopped at the last box and studied it.

"Nothing changes, does it?" Logan said.

I wanted to ignore him more, but it was getting harder to do so. I was in his house in any case. And I was walking around, uninvited, in his house library.

"What doesn't change?" I asked, humoring him, though my gut told me to just slap him and walk away. That was the least he deserved for ditching me at my junior prom, forcing me to call my mother to give me a ride home after everyone left and I was still there alone. Sure, Logan. You'll be right back. That was the last time I believed that lie.

"Party is going, and I find you in the library. You were never one for crowds," Logan replied, stepping closer. He was finally close enough that I could see his violet eyes in the room's dim light. Along with his magical house, he had magical eyes. All the girls would talk about his strangely colored eyes. They weren't blue, but truly violet. Those violet eyes were busy studying me with a hint of humor in them.

I wanted to deny that was me, but I couldn't with him. I had dated him for two years, and he knew me quite well. At least, he knew the former me quite well. My reply ended up being a shrug. I looked back down at the nearest book for a distraction. I stared hard at the words on the page. The elegant golden lines swirled around the pages in Celtic knots. Even this book felt like I could read it, if I knew how.

I finally looked up at him. He was still staring at me. It was a bit unnerving, actually. It was as if he was looking for a secret on me. I had secrets all right, and a few more now than when we were together, but I still wasn't about to tell him about them. In fact, I couldn't tell anyone about them. If I told someone I could travel through time, I knew exactly where I'd end up: locked away in a mental ward. People would think I was crazy. Heck, even I thought it was crazy, but that didn't matter now. I wanted to get Seth back, so, crazy or not, I was going to time travel back to find him.

"Maybe some things do change," Logan added quietly after assessing me.

I turned away from Logan and his intense stare and walked over to the large picture windows on the wall next to me. I looked out over the evening Chicago skyline. Lights blinked all around and up into the air on the tall buildings. It was a city horizon. I looked up into the sky and could only see a few faint stars. I missed Minnesota at that moment, and I missed all the stars. I never knew how many stars were in the sky until I moved away from the city.

Logan slowly trailed behind me. I watched in the dim reflection on the window as he stopped behind me. I felt the heat from him being too close before he stepped beside me.

"Is it possible that we can start over?" he said quietly.

"Start over?" I asked. That wasn't what I was expecting to hear from him. I was glad I wasn't drinking. I probably would have spit it all over him.

"I'd like to be your friend, Mari. I've missed you these past few years. I know that I hurt you pretty bad, and I deserve every hateful thing you've ever thought of me, but I was hoping that there was a chance we could just start over, as friends," Logan watched the city skyline with me. He was poised and collected. Like he had practiced this conversation before.

A weird bit of déjà vu came over me. It was as if I had had this exact conversation with Logan. It wasn't in his library, but somewhere else. He asked then if we could start over just the same way as he did now. I shook off the feeling. This was the first time I had seen him in over two years. Maybe I had a dream about it. Probably right after we broke up, and I was still desperately in love with him. That had to be it.

"Friends?" I asked. "Just friends?"

"Yes, just friends." Logan turned and gave me his million-dollar smile. "Unless you want more," he suggested with a grin. "I'm just kidding," he added at my hesitation.

I wanted to say *no* as his eyes were hinting that there was something behind his "just friends" comment, but I didn't have a reason to keep him away any longer. I wasn't still pining over him. In fact, I had moved on completely. While he would always make my stomach flutter a little, he was my first love after all, I didn't feel the need to be with him. When I fell asleep at night, I dreamed of being in Seth's arms now. When I woke in the morning, I thought of Seth. I was completely in love with Seth.

"Sure," I replied with a shrug.

Logan smiled and looked back to the city. I didn't know why that would make him happy. I was going back to school in a day or two, and would be miles away, but I wasn't about to ask. Something in his eyes told me there was more behind his question than I wanted to know. One thing had not changed in all the time that had passed, Logan Jones was still planning something.

CHAPTER 3

TIME TRAVEL TRY

"**Welcome home, roomie,**" Sim greeted me while I pushed the door open with my foot because my hands were full of stuff I was bringing back. I was surprised to see Sim. She had actually made it back before me.

My first semester in college had been great because Sim was my roommate. It was nice to get back and see a friendly face. She wasn't going to tease me about being at Morton or in Minnesota. She was genuinely happy to see me. I welcomed the change from being home and seeing my old friends. They would always be my friends, but Sim would be the one that understood the *me* that I became at college.

The drive had been long and gave me way too much time to think. All I could do was wonder about Seth. Why didn't he make it back? Was he safe? Could I go back to that exact moment and save him? So many of my questions were still unanswered, I needed to find a way to control the time travel and make it to him, but I didn't want to just run off as I had before. I was naïve to think I could just go to the past and walk away from it with him. I knew better now. I had learned my lesson. The past isn't something you mess with lightly. I needed a plan, and for that I needed Ty. He would help me. Maybe he even knew what went wrong.

I stumbled across the room to my bed and dropped everything. It was nice to be home. After living in the dorms for months, the little room we shared felt more and more like where I belonged than Chicago, and Amy just solidified the feeling by dragging me off to a party. My room back in Chicago would always be home, but this is where I lived my own way. It had been hard to say goodbye to my grandfather, but he reassured me that he would be fine. He was a tough old man, and he was right, but he missed my mother as much as I did. I had to get her back for his sake, if not mine.

"Did you have a good break?" Sim asked hesitantly. "You know, the first one without your mom," she added quietly.

I nodded. I forgot for a moment that everyone thought my mother died this summer. It was nice that the goddess didn't erase her completely like she'd done with Seth. I must have told Sim that same story in the alternative universe that happened when she left. I had been slowly regaining memories for the past few days. I remembered how the past happened with Seth in it, and then some memories were starting to show the same situations without him in it. I hated having two memories of most events in my life. It was confusing and annoying at the same time. Most of my memories were identical to my previous memories, but with little details that were different because Seth supposedly didn't exist. Also, anything relating to my mother was different. It would take time to sort through everything, the fake and the real memories.

"We survived. How was your break?" I asked back. Obviously she didn't want to upset me with talk about my mother. And yes, it was upsetting me. I didn't just lose her over the summer; I had lost her only a week ago. The feelings were still too raw.

"Typical Singh family Thanksgiving. My parents try way too hard to be *American*," she said with an eye roll.

I could imagine that. Her parents seemed very Indian from when I met them, her mother only wore saris and her dad wore a turban every day, but all the stories Sim told me from her childhood made them out to be ultra-patriotic.

As I unpacked, I made sure my new carnelian lines were visible. Sim didn't even say a word. It was strange as the lines were getting darker in color, and I was sure they stood out. My skin was quite pale and I burned easily in sunlight so I never had a tan. The carnelian lines were now a reddish-brown color.

"Have you talked to Ty at all?" she asked. She was trying to just throw it in the conversation, but I knew Sim well enough by now. Her voice even cracked a little when she said his name.

In my old memories Sim and Ty were my two best friends, but my new memories have Sim with more than a little crush on Ty. It was weird to see life both times. It wasn't that I didn't want my two best college friends to get together. In fact, they'd make a cute couple, but even I knew Ty's life was a little too complicated for him to have a serious relationship, and I didn't want Sim hurt. Now I wasn't really sure how to handle the new memories.

"I haven't talked to Ty yet. You know, no cell phone," I answered, pulling my sleeve back to expose the whole line. Sim watched me and said nothing.

"Exactly. What's wrong with him? It's abnormal to not have one," Sim complained. She wouldn't have called him if he did have one. When Sim really liked a guy, she got very shy.

I got the very distinct feeling that Sim couldn't see the lines on my arm. I was going to ask her how to lie about them to people, but if Sim couldn't see them, I was going to bet everyone else not connected to time traveling and the goddess couldn't either. It was one more secret, but an invisible secret is much easier to keep than a real one.

We soon began talking about random things as I unpacked. After the long drive I was exhausted. We chatted until I needed to sleep because I was too tired to talk any more. I had plans for an early morning. Ty would be up early, and I would be, too.

All our talking made me feel normal again, but it was far from the truth. I'd never be normal, and I could never be happy without Seth. I needed to be with him in his time, or mine, and I was going to find a way how. I doubted Ty could teach me how to time travel, but I couldn't leave him out. He was as much a part of this as I was. Together we would get everyone back. I knew it.

I woke long before Sim would even crack an eye open. Sometimes it was good that she wasn't a morning person, as I didn't need to come up with an excuse for visiting Ty early in the morning. From our talk last night, she was interested in him, and I really didn't want her to think that there was anything like that between us. She had no memories of Seth, so she couldn't remember that he was the one I was looking for every time I walked on campus. I wouldn't see him, but the memories of the erased past were still stronger for me than the new past. Those all felt like a dream.

As quietly as I could, I quickly dressed warmly and headed out into the light snow. Campus was completely dead at early morning hours the last day of the break, like it should have been. If I wasn't set on my goal, I would have been sleeping in, too. We now had a week of classes and finals before the semester was done. Everyone was taking this slight break in the hustle of the end of a semester. I couldn't take a break. I was on a mission. I had to learn how to go into the past to bring back Seth and my mother.

I hurried across the frozen, silent campus trying not to think of my old memories. Everything was packed in my mind in a big jumble. New memories and old memories of the same situation were both there, and I was beginning to question some of them. They were similar, yet still different. It was just too confusing. There were new memories, but since they were fake, I didn't care to remember them. I tried not to let them take over. Seth was real. My first semester of college, where I fell in love with him, was real. The other stuff was not. I kept repeating that to myself as I walked.

It didn't take me long to make it to their house with my feet on autopilot. It was the same as when Seth first left. I had been there too many times to not be able to make it there without thinking. It was his house, but still I could feel the joy of the three best friends missing. There were only a couple lights on. It looked sad. It felt empty now.

"I never really took you for this early of a morning person," a deep, gruff voice said from behind me.

I turned and threw myself into Ty's arms. Until that moment, I still doubted that even he made it back. The goddess took everyone from me. It was hard enough to deal with the loss of my mother and my boyfriend, I figured it was possible Mr. Sangre misspoke, and I'd have to deal with the loss of my best guy friend, too. Sim and Ty made college for me. My world wouldn't have been the same without them both in it. College would have never been the same.

"You're really here," was all I could reply. I didn't want to let go, like he would just melt into the past like everyone else.

Ty patted my back. "Yes, I'm really here, and you're really frozen. Let's get inside."

I let go and tried to discreetly wipe my eyes. I couldn't help getting a little misty. I really thought I was left completely alone. They had left me alone before, and I felt like it would be that way again. They were from the past. They had to go back at some time, but I just didn't want that yet, or maybe ever. Someday I would be alone in the future, but for now I had Ty. I wasn't alone.

Ty opened the door to the house and pretended not to see my tears. I liked that part of him. He let me be a girl and never teased me about it when I had a moment here or there. I followed him inside as he went upstairs to his room. At least the house looked lived-in again, even though I knew Seth and Dee weren't here. It was harder to come back to than the first time they had left, seeing the place without them. There was nothing left of the three boys, and the house looked immaculately new that time. Not this time at least. I let out another sigh. That meant that Ty was really here. Even if I saw him walking in front of me, I figured that I could have just been hallucinating from the cold.

"It's kind of weird," Ty said, sitting down on his bed. I sat on his window seat across from him. He was still in his running clothes, but I obviously had interrupted him. He wasn't even sweaty.

"I know. I keep getting confused," I replied. I tucked my feet under me. I guess I was a little frozen. That was the bad thing about walking around in a Minnesota winter. You didn't want to let your mind wander and stay out too long, or you'd end up like I was: just a bit cold.

"Exactly. It's like I have two memories of everything. Well, most everything. And I don't know which one is real sometimes," Ty answered, describing exactly what I was feeling. "You should see how strange it is to have two memories of the same football game. It feels like I drank the funky water and everything is just blurred together."

I laughed for the first time in a week. I was grateful to have Ty around. He was the only one that could understand exactly what I was feeling, funky water and all.

"Oh, I know which ones are real. I find the second ones more annoying than anything. It's like someone hijacked my brain without my permission. I mean, who has the right to change my memories?" I complained, picking up a chocolate-colored pillow and threading my fingers through the tassels. Even his room was exactly the same as before, decorated in brown tones.

"Exactly what I was thinking. It's like my first memories weren't good enough and someone is trying to make new ones. Why didn't I get to choose the memories I wanted to have?" Ty replied, taking off his shoes. Guess he wasn't going for a run now.

"Oh, I'm choosing, even if it's a dream world now. They are much better than the new ones," I replied, and Ty smiled. He knew exactly what I was talking about: Seth. I couldn't help the blush that crept into my cheeks. I didn't mean just those memories, but yes, being kissed by Seth was better than any of the replacements.

"I don't think I could ever get used to this. I mean, think of how Mr. Sangre deals with this all the time? It would drive me nuts," Ty said.

"But weren't you guys the first ones he took on to pretend to be his own children?" I asked. I didn't know that this was something he dealt with. I thought he brought people into the past or future, and then left them to do what they needed to do.

"Yes, but that was because he didn't want to oversee us constantly for as long as we needed to be here. Normally people only come for a few days, or maybe weeks. He checks in on them often, and watches over them. I guess it's part of his job, making sure they stay safe and don't change major historical events and all. But with us, we were told we would be here for years. He decided to just call us his children and be able to go on dealing with his other travelers," Ty explained.

"Then every person he helps travel, he knows what they are doing and when they will go back?" I had assumed it was more you stayed until your mission was done. It changed everything if people were given a set time. I had to wonder who set the time. Was it the goddess, or the person bringing them back?

"I guess," Ty replied. Then he realized my question and added, "Why?"

"Do you think if I bring someone back that they will have a limited time if they don't go through Mr. Sangre?" I replied. Could I keep Seth and my mother in the future, and not have to worry about them disappearing?

"You're going to go get them?" Ty asked.

"Yes. I can't leave them in the past," I replied. "I need to learn how to time travel." I wanted to see how Ty would respond. He leaned over to the side table and grabbed something.

When he turned back, Ty grinned. "And I'll be beside you the whole way." He held up his own piece of chalcedony.

I grinned back at him. At first I had some doubts that Ty would want to time travel. I had only a glimpse of his life in the past, and he was far better off here in the future. In the past he was a slave to Seth's family. Here, he was free.

He must have seen the relief on my face as he set down the stone and joined me on the window seat.

"What? Did you think I'd let you go off on adventures on your own? I promised Seth I'd take care of you, and you're the best friend I've made in this time. I couldn't let you run off alone. You have the power to direct travel, and I have the power to go with you," Ty explained. "I think it works out perfectly."

"I know I can direct travel, but that's the main problem. I have the ability, but I don't know how," I complained. At least he was on board with my plan to time travel again. Now I just needed to learn how.

"Couldn't you talk to Logan?" Ty asked, looking out the window behind us. Someone was standing on the snow covered beach.

"Logan?" I repeated. There was only one Logan I knew, and I had happily left him back in Chicago, or so I thought.

"Logan Jones, as in Mr. Sangre's son," Ty said as if it were obvious. He knew something I did not, but I got the feeling I was supposed to. "You know, the one that is going to school here now in place of Seth."

Memories flooded my mind instantly. I hadn't thought of the fake past since it wasn't mine, but now I saw it all. Instead of Seth leading the football team, it was now Logan. Instead of Seth pursuing me through my first semester in college, it was Logan. And then my sense of déjà vu over Thanksgiving at the party was suddenly clear. When Logan asked to start over as friends, he had already asked me that once. I just hadn't remembered then that Logan had moved into my life in place of Seth. He had to have known, but I didn't. Thins had just gotten a bit more complicated, but it did explain more to me.

Pain and anger filled me as I wrestled with the two pasts in my mind. I didn't want replacement memories, and I didn't want any with Logan Jones in them. I wanted my memories of Seth back as the only memories. I didn't like Logan anymore. I liked Seth. Logan was playing with fire if he thought he could weasel his way back into my love life, because it wasn't going to work. If Logan swooped in and took my memories away, he should be able to fix it. I hated having to talk to him, but it looked like I would have to set him straight.

"Where is he?" I asked Ty. Ty pointed to the window

and the frozen shoreline outside.

I began to put my jacket, hat, and scarf back on to brave the winter weather. Ty stood beside me and watched while he was debating what to do.

"I'm going to head back to the dorms after I talk to him. Sim will be wondering where I am," I told Ty. "Do we still have a tutor session tomorrow?" Old past and new past were a bit complicated, but most of everything with Ty was still the same.

"Yea," Ty replied, still carefully watching me. He was unsure if he should stop me going out to confront Logan or not, or if he should come with me. Full protection mode was on.

"Don't worry," I replied to his look. I had to smile. It was nice to have at least one thing the same. Ty was still my friend, and was still protective of me. "I know Logan Jones quite well. I need him to understand that no matter what memories he gave me, or anyone else, I still love Seth."

Ty seemed to relax a little.

"Fine, but don't do anything to piss him off. I don't need him sending you off to some other time, I'd have to follow to rescue you," Ty replied in all seriousness. "I heard stories and have seen Mr. Sangre yell at him more than once for doing things like that. It seems that whenever someone did something Logan didn't like, he'd just whisk them away and drop them off in a different time. Mr. Sangre has spent a large part of the past two years cleaning up his messes. I don't need you turning into another mess."

It was my turn to give him the questioning look. Logan wasn't like that, at least never around me. I hadn't seen him get mad once in the two years we dated. He was the type of guy that all of the other guys loved to be around, and the girls loved him even more. I couldn't imagine him doing something vindictive.

"But you know that wouldn't matter with me," I replied, pointing to my arm as the key to the problem. "I'd come right back." Ty nodded and relaxed a little. "Unfortunately, even if I knew how to push him into some other time he would probably come back, too."

Ty laughed. I was being serious, but Ty thought it was a joke. I smiled, but it wasn't funny. I thought I had gotten rid of Logan when I dumped him, but now I was beginning to think it wasn't that easy. He tried to get me back after we broke up, but I just stopped accepting his calls. It really was that easy, or so I thought. Now I had to wonder.

If he was like Mr. Sangre, he could travel through time. Did he really leave me alone when I thought I had been left alone? How many other secrets was he hiding? I thought I knew Logan, but now I wasn't sure. Ty seemed a bit scared of him, and if what he said was true, with good reason. Maybe Logan wasn't the same person I thought I knew. One thing I did know though was that I didn't want him in my life romantically, and he needed to be told that. There had to be no question behind it. Logan wasn't Seth, and never would be.

I went downstairs and out the side doorway onto the beach. The icy wind blew, and I pulled my scarf up over my face more. I was going to really have to get used to the early winter up in the North Country. By now Chicago would be cold, but not this cold. There was a light cover of snow on the sand, which was a stark contrast to the waves that still lapped the shoreline. The shoreline was still liquid, but I couldn't wait until it wasn't. I was a little excited to see the edges of the lake freeze like Sim had told me about. At least there was a little bit of fun I could expect from the weather I was going to have to endure until April.

Up the shoreline was a silhouette. I walked briskly across the sand, but I had to slow as I neared. It was as if

Seth was still there. The silhouette was his size and shape, looking off to the water just as I had found Seth many times. The sun was rising, and the person was only a black shadow. For a moment I could pretend it was Seth. A small part of me hoped everything was wrong and that he was somehow back with me. I wanted to shout and run to him. I wanted to throw my arms around his neck and tell him how much I loved him. I wanted him to be really there. It wasn't true, but I couldn't help what my heart wanted. As I got closer, it became clear it wasn't Seth when the person's hair wasn't the dark red I was hoping for. Instead, I found the dusty, blondish-brown hair I was still way too familiar with.

"You can't just replace him," I said, not waiting for Logan to turn toward me.

I had hoped the cold air would cool my temper a little, especially after Ty's hesitation that Logan would send me off to another time, but it didn't. Logan had just pushed his way into my life, and not even as the friend he claimed he wanted to start over as. He was trying to be my love interest, and I still wasn't interested in him. I had moved on. He needed to be told that straight up.

Logan turned and stared at me with his serious violet eyes. There was a slight smile on his lips.

"I didn't do a good enough job making everything the same?" Logan asked. "I thought we made a cute couple. In fact, I'm pretty sure your roommate thinks that, too."

Unfortunately, he did a great job making it all the same, with him in place of Seth. That was the problem.

"We're not a couple," I snapped back. "I love Seth, not you." I meant for the words to sting him, but didn't actually expect to see it on his face. He looked hurt by my words. We had broken up two years ago. I had moved on. I thought he had, too.

"Ahh, but we're a couple here. Well, maybe not officially, but everyone thinks we will be soon." Logan was back to smiling as he talked, but his smile seemed different. I looked closer at him. He even seemed different.

"Logan," I protested. He smiled even brighter, like he enjoyed hearing me draw out his name. "Back at your house, you asked to be friends. I thought you meant like long-distance friends that saw each other once a year. I was fine with that. A friend is all I want. I can't date you again. I really do like Seth," I said with a little less anger.

"And Seth is in the past, thousands of years in the past," Logan reminded me. "You don't think you should move on here in the future?" He was still making a play for me.

"I can't move on," I admitted. Logan was the last person I wanted to confess that to, but it just came out. It was something I couldn't explain, but I needed to be with Seth.

A hurt look crossed his face again, but Logan turned back into the sun to avoid my stare.

"Well, you better face up and move on. The goddess made it very clear that Seth won't be back in this time. He has a role to play in the past, not here," Logan replied.

I sucked in a breath. Seth wouldn't be back. I thought I could just go into the past and bring him back, but maybe it wouldn't be that easy.

"I'm not moving on, and I'm not leaving Seth behind," I replied. It didn't matter what Logan said. I couldn't live the rest of my life wondering how it would have turned out with Seth. I needed the chance to find out.

Logan turned back to me. "Mari, the goddess is in charge. If she says he can't come back, then he can't come back. I wish I could say something else, but that's the way it works. She has the power, and no matter who we think should or shouldn't be in a particular time, we don't get the choice." His words were a bit bitter.

"We'll see about that," I replied and turned on my heels to walk away. Thankfully, he didn't stop me. The goddess may have a say as to who she helps, but I had the power to travel now. And with Dee's stone, I could choose who I helped. I just hoped the goddess wouldn't send them back right after I got them here.

I passed the Sangre house on my walk back to school, and as I did, Ty popped out the doorway. He was fully dressed and had his bag with him.

"Heading back to the dorms?" I asked.

He shook his head. "No, we need to stop at the library and try something."

"We?" I asked. He looked a little shaken, but happy. He followed behind me as I crossed the deserted road outside their house.

"Well that's what you just told me to do. We can use one of those little private study rooms and give the time travel stuff a chance," Ty replied. I stopped on the other side of the road, and he stopped beside me.

"What?" I asked. I could feel my mouth hanging open and there was nothing I could do about it.

"You just popped into my living room while I was sitting there studying. You said we should go to the library to study and give the time travel a try," Ty replied as he started to walk. I tripped a little as I tried to catch up to him. I had to learn how to time travel, but it seemed a bit sudden of a start.

Ty laughed at my stumble. "Yeah, well you should have seen me. I guess you'll see me in a few minutes, but yes, I didn't think we'd be trying today. Heck, we haven't even made a plan yet of what to do to get everyone back. Seth and Dee will come back, I'm sure, but how do we get them back without the goddess stones? You have one and I do, and it seems Seth's no longer works."

I guess I had forgotten a few details to tell him since I got back.

"Yeah, well I have two stones," I answered. It was Ty's turn to stare at me.

"I took my grandfather's carnelian stone, which turned out to be Seth's. The goddess kind of gave it to me forever." I pulled up my coat sleeve to show Ty the red lines. They were getting darker each day.

"That's the carnelian?" Ty asked, stopping to look closer at the lines. He could see the lines even if Sim couldn't.

"Yeah. Dee didn't give me a chance to respond after he gave me his stone. Now I have two stones, but that still isn't enough." I rolled my sleeve back down to protect my arm from the cold. It was strange. I did it out of habit, but once the sleeve was back down I realized my arm wasn't even cold. The stone kept me warm.

"If you have two stones, and I have one, then couldn't you just go back to get them both and bring them back? I could wait here, or we could both just go back and bring one home at a time," Ty suggested.

"They're not the only ones I need to bring back," I replied. Ty didn't ask right away. He waited for me to explain.

We had made it to the woods between east and west campus now. The bare trees were different than the fall foliage on the day Seth saved me, and it was too late to not fall for him. That day I had to admit the truth. Now, it was so different. All my new memories were different. I needed to get him back, but I couldn't leave my mother there.

"The goddess took my mother back," I finally told Ty.

"What?" Ty asked, grabbing my arms and turning me to face him. "She did what?"

"She took my mother back to the past," I said a second time before the tears started.

Ty pulled me to his chest and hugged me as I cried. I didn't mean to cry, and I thought I didn't have any more tears left, but they still came pouring out. Of anyone I met at college, Ty would be the one to know how much my mother meant to me. We often talked about our parents. He missed his greatly as he had been parted from them since he was four. I only had a week to get used to my loss.

"I'm very sorry, Mari." As my tears dried and I pulled back, Ty asked, "How could she just take your mother away?"

"It was part of their agreement. Once I could travel into the past on my own, my mother had to return," I answered as we began to walk again. I sniffled a little. Ty kept his arm around my shoulder. "I need to go back and get her. She doesn't belong to that time. She has spent most of her life here in the present. She belongs here."

"Easy enough. We first bring her back, and then deal with Seth and Dee," Ty said. He was certain saving my mom was the priority, I couldn't doubt him. Ty was truly a best friend.

Ty led the way into the library and to the fourth floor study area. I fished my keys out from my bag and unlocked an empty room. There were some perks of being a tutor, beyond meeting my best guy friend and my new boyfriend who currently resided in ancient history somewhere. There was the free access to quiet study rooms, which were perfect to discreetly use and plan an unbelievable journey. I wasn't giving up on Seth yet for being my boyfriend. Heck, he had even asked me in the past to marry him, so maybe he'll be even more than a boyfriend where he comes from.

"We first need to figure out the time travel, and then we need to make a plan," I said as we closed the door. "I can't go back knowing nothing of the time. I know my mother was a princess, but where? What were her people called? Where did she live? Who was in charge? What were the rules? How do I go about finding her? I have so many more questions. I needed to know more this time. I'm not going blindly into the past again. The more we know, the easier it will be to get everyone home."

"I know you couldn't use computers before, but I wonder without Seth here, can you do it now? I'm not of his people. Maybe it will work now," Ty suggested.

That was something I didn't think about. I wasn't technically messing with the past when Seth wasn't here. Even if Ty was from the past, he was not Egyptian, I could learn more without affecting his future, hopefully. Only Seth and Dee were actually Egyptian. I could learn more about Seth and his time, and there was no reason not to.

I took my coat and bag and placed them on the table. Ty did the same. First, I had to try the time travel back to the moment earlier in the day when I told him to come to the study rooms with me. I sat down across from him.

"How did we do it?" I asked, getting right to it. Time travel was easy when I was going back to Seth. There was something about him that drew me. All I had to do was follow that string, and *poof,* I was right there with him. I had no clue how to do anything else with the time travel.

"I don't know. It wasn't like we talked much. I was studying on the couch when suddenly you were standing in front of me. You told me to hurry up and come back with you so that we could do this," Ty explained. *Great.* He wasn't going to be much help.

I stood and began to pace around the small boxed room. There was a window to peek into the room on the wall beside the solid door, but it only allowed the person to see the study table. I stopped behind the door and out of view.

I was nervous to even try time travel this time. During my previous time travel experience, I didn't think about it. I just went with my gut. It felt right. But now I had to think. I had to do this correctly to end up in the right place at the right time. It was reassuring to know I already did it, but I still didn't know how. I tried to think of Ty like I had to travel to Seth. If I thought of him hard enough, maybe I'd end up with him in the past. I closed my eyes and waited a moment, but I didn't go anywhere. There were no fuzzies, and I knew I was still in the present.

"I need something to go by," I said to Ty. Ty paused for a moment and thought.

"I was sitting on the couch. The TV was on, but I wasn't watching it. It was some basketball game for background noise. I had just finished my bio homework and was pulling out my math homework. It is due tomorrow. You know, one of those great profs that like to make you work over holidays. I got my book out." Ty dug through his bag and grabbed the faded, navy blue book.

I pictured the Sangre house as he described it and could even picture Ty on the couch. It wasn't like I hadn't seen him sitting there over a dozen times in my multiple pasts. I felt the fuzzies as he placed his book on the table. I didn't have time to speak as I was instantly in the Sangre living room.

"Ty," I said, surprised to see Ty sitting on the couch and not in the study room.

His mouth dropped in shock, and he didn't reply. I had to stifle my laugh. Yep, he looked just like I felt not even ten minutes ago.

"Mari?" he asked, like it wasn't me that had just popped into his house. Maybe he thought I was an alien.

"Yes. Me, Mari. You, Ty," I replied in my best robot voice. Ty didn't even smile. "Yes, Ty it's me," I said more normally.

"Why? How?" he stuttered.

"Well, in ten minutes you'll walk back with me to school and the library to one of the study rooms. We'll try it then and you'll help me do this," I replied, pointing to myself and then the room.

"You will time travel?" Ty replied, slowly catching on.

"Yes, with your help, and as long as you get your butt out there to walk back with me. Otherwise, I was just going back to my room," I answered.

Ty stood and hastily grabbed his books to throw into his bag while he was sliding on his shoes. As he was putting his coat on, I saw a figure through the glass window on the kitchen door, Logan. I rushed back to the living room.

"Hurry up," I told him as Ty zipped his coat and grabbed his bag. I looked down and saw the same navy book he pulled out in the library on the coffee table. "And don't forget your math book. You have homework due tomorrow."

Ty took his bag and grinned at me. "I knew we could do this."

Ty was out the door, and I hung back as I watched myself walk by. It was strange to see myself, to say the least, but I did worry about all that science fiction stuff about being in the same place at the same time would cause some sort of damage. I watched as they walked to the road and knew exactly what was being said. I went back to the living room. It was as good a time as any to go back.

I thought of the study room and Ty's face as he saw me fade. Closing my eyes, I pictured everything clearly and waited for the fuzzies. *Nothing*. I pictured it in more vivid details, the bags strewn on the table, the book in his hand, the faded white walls pressed to my back. I waited. *Nothing again*. I wasn't going anywhere. Now, this was a problem.

I flopped onto the couch. What was I to do? I was stuck in the past and had no clue how to get back. This wasn't a good idea after all. Sure I could go someplace, but it did no good if I couldn't return. I laid my head back and sighed. This wasn't as easy as we pictured it to be. I needed help, and only the person I could think of to help was the goddess. I wasn't exactly happy with her after she took away the people I love, therefore I was more willing to just sit and wait. I had traveled into the future, now I just needed to find a way to go back.

"If you're here and I saw you walk away with Ty, is it safe to assume that you're not the current Mari that just yelled at me moments ago?" Logan asked from behind me. Again, I was startled since I hadn't heard him enter the room.

I sat up and looked at him. I was still mad at him, and he didn't deserve a reply. I shrugged and lay back against the couch. I closed my eyes and tried again to picture the study room. The sooner I left, the better. I really didn't want to be in an empty house with Logan; especially a Logan who wasn't accepting that I was in love with Seth.

"Looks like you could use some help," Logan suggested. His voice was getting closer. He was walking over to the couch. I still didn't open my eyes or reply. "How much of the stone did you use up to travel?" he asked.

I finally opened my eyes. I had to. I had no clue what he was even talking about. He knew more about how to time travel than I did, but I didn't want his help. Even the little bits he was now giving me were, annoyingly, making me want to ask more. Logan laughed at my lack of response.

"Did the goddess tell you nothing? All the other ones she gave lessons to, and here she lets her last one be all alone. I have no idea what she's playing at. Where did she place the stone in you? Can you see it?" Logan asked, sitting beside me. The things he was saying were a little confusing to me, but I had to answer his question. I wanted to go home, and it seemed like maybe if I talked to him, I could get away from him.

I pulled back my sleeve. I needed some help, and since he was offering I would have to take what I could get. Help from Logan always came at a price, though.

Logan's eyes got big as he looked at my arm. "That's the stone?" he asked.

"Yes," I replied, unsure why he was surprised. He was the one that knew the stone was within me. "And?" I prompted, looking for an answer.

Logan picked up my hand and turned it gently over to look at the lines that crisscrossed around my wrist. Except for the few lines that radiated from my wrist, it looked like a red bracelet.

"That sneaky devil." Logan chuckled as he examined the lines closely.

"What do you mean?" I asked.

"Nothing." Logan shook his head and continued to hold my arm. Since he was no longer inspecting it, I pulled it back out of his grasp. "Where do the lines normally go to?" he asked, smiling at my response of pulling away from him.

"Almost to my elbow and down to my fingers," I replied, pointing to where one each ended. Logan nodded.

"Well, I'd have to guess that until they show up again, you won't be going anywhere," Logan replied.

"Have to guess?" I replied, somewhat in shock, and somewhat mocking him. He acted like he knew what was going on, and now he was guessing.

"Well, she's never exactly put a stone in someone like that before," Logan replied. "Most of the time she puts the whole stone just under the skin. It fades when used up, and grows darker when it's ready to be used again. I'm guessing your lines are like that."

55

"She's never done this before?" I repeated what he already stated. I knew there were others like me, but I never considered who or where they were. "How many people like me have you run across?"

"A few dozen over the years," Logan replied with a shrug.

Logan was my age, nineteen. How could he have seen a few dozen when they were born very rarely? Had he traveled that much? Yes, Logan wasn't the person I knew two years ago.

"I can teach you how to use that stone," Logan added again.

"For what price?" I asked. It had to be asked. Logan was turning out to have a much larger past that I ever imagined, and he wasn't the person I remembered.

"I don't have a price. How about we say, I teach you for a future favor?" he asked, mystery and seduction laced his voice. I didn't like the sound of that.

I involuntarily shivered. My gut told me I had something he wanted, something he couldn't name now, because he knew I would say no. He had gone to so much trouble to make himself central in my life again. I wasn't sure if I could trust him now. Ty's voice rang in my head. Ty, the warrior from the past, was wary of Logan. He wasn't the same boy I dated two years ago. Then again, I don't know if he ever was. My old and new memories were at odds.

I shook my head *no*. I couldn't agree to that. There was no guarantee what his price would be. I had a feeling there were secrets in Logan Jones I didn't want to know.

"Come on, Mari," Logan pleaded, some of his old boyishness shining through his intense stare. "If I don't teach you, who will? It will take forever to learn on your own. I can teach you, you can save your boy, and then all you will owe me is a small favor in the future."

"I don't trust you," I replied honestly. Well, maybe that

wasn't the best thing to say to him now. If he did send me into the past, there was no way I could go anywhere.

Logan laughed. "What is there not to trust? I'm the same Logan you dated two years ago. You trusted me then, why not now?"

"I didn't really know you then, did I?" I asked in reply.

"Didn't know me? I knew you, and I have a feeling you still know me," he replied seductively. I shook my head and shuffled over on the couch a few inches. I did remember our time together, but how could I not? He was the first boy I ever kissed. I would remember that forever.

"If you knew me that well, you would have known that I wouldn't have appreciated you coming into my life and pretending to be my boyfriend. I don't like my memories messed with, and I'm not going to pretend to be in love with you like I was with Seth." I stood and made my way toward the doorway. I wasn't going to sit around with Logan while I waited for the stone to come back. I was sure now I never knew him. As I got to the doorway, Logan finally replied.

"I knew that if I let your memories be altered as they would have without Seth around, you wouldn't have been happy with the results. You would have never been friends with Ty. You would have never done CRUSH, and your friendship with Sim would have been completely different," Logan said quietly. I had to stop to listen to him. "I put myself into your memories, in Seth's place, to keep everything almost the same for you. I knew you would hate the results of the past changing, and I did my best to keep as much the same as I could. I still know you, Mari. I still love you. I will never stop, no matter who you love instead of me. I knew how much you'd be hurt, and I did the only thing I could to keep it from being worse."

That wasn't what I expected to hear from him. I figured his only reason was to get back into my life, but it wasn't according to him. Still, it didn't change anything.

As nice as his words were, they were still just words. Every moment I spent with him I now had to question. What was real and what was not? I still didn't trust Logan. He wasn't who I thought he was. He never had been.

I continued through the doorway and up the staircase. I planned on hiding out in Ty's room, it wasn't like he was coming back any time soon, but my feet led me down the hallway a bit. I opened the door, knowing that it wouldn't be the same. I had already been in the room with Seth gone. The sea theme with the blue and white was gone, and the room was decorated in just plain white now. It seemed clean and sterile, but it was still his room. I still had memories of lying in his bed the night after he saved me. He was there with me. His arms had made me feel safe. I missed him so much more now. I sat down on the bed. It was still Seth's bed, no matter where he was.

I lay down and looked at the ceiling. I wanted to feel his arms around me again, I wanted him to be with me. I needed help, but I wasn't sure who to ask. Mr. Sangre said he couldn't help me, Logan said he could for a favor, and Ty was as clueless as I was, even though he had time traveled just as many times as I had. There was only one person left to ask.

"Goddess," I whispered as I stared at the ceiling more.

A warm breeze flitted into the room even though the door and windows were closed. It was her. I could feel her even if I couldn't see her.

"I need help," I added, waiting for her to appear. She did not. I sighed. Yep, not even the goddess could help me. I was truly alone on this.

"You need no help," a voice said from around me. Again, she wasn't in a shape that I could see, like she had been in my first conversations, but she was in the room. I began to wonder if there was a reason now that I could not see her. I'd have to wonder later as she was with me now and I needed answers.

"I jumped into the past for just minutes, and now can't get back," I told her. I did need help, and she was my last resort.

"As with any travels, you just need to wait. Then you can go back," the goddess replied.

"But I don't know how," I replied. I truly didn't know how to travel in time.

"Then how did you get here?" she asked, floating around the room as her voice moved with her.

I had just thought about it, and then I was there. That wasn't *knowing how*. It just happened. I couldn't explain that to her. There was nothing that I did or thought. There was nothing I could repeat or do again.

"You're making too much of this. It is simple. You don't need someone to teach you; you need to believe in yourself," the goddess answered, reading my thoughts.

I looked to my arm. The lines had grown but weren't full yet. I'd have no choice but to wait as she said. Maybe it was that simple. Her presence left the room and the warm wind was fading with her.

"Wait," I called to her. "Why?" I asked, doing my best to hold back the tears. The goddess made you feel warm and happy in her presence, and I thought she was on the side of the good guys. The fact that she would take my mother away seemed wrong to me.

"Why?" she repeated, as if she didn't know what I was questioning.

"Why take them away? Why leave me without the people I love?" I asked in barely a whisper.

"Oh, child," the goddess replied, coming back into the room in full force. I could make out the outline of her as she stood near the bed. "If I could have left your mother here, I would have, but that isn't the way it works. She was born in the past. She had to return."

"Why? She spent fifteen years in the past, and twenty here. She belonged more to the future than the past. You sent her back to relive what she ran away from," I protested. I had many times in the past week imagined what my mother's life was now like. She ran away from that life to protect me, and now she was back living it. It wasn't fair.

"She went back to almost twenty years from when she left. She will not relive her past," the goddess replied, trying to calm my worst fears. "And I'm sorry, but that's the way time works. You can't take one from one time and let them live their lives out in another time. It isn't right. I gave my power into the stones so that mankind could get help, not so that they could run away from their problems."

"And what am I to do now? My mother is gone, my boyfriend is gone, and I'm left stuck in the future by a power I don't know how to use." I couldn't help but complain about the situation, since this was partially the goddess' fault. Logan said she had trained everyone else before me, but not me. If she had trained me, then maybe I wouldn't be in the predicament I was in now.

"My agreement with your mother was that once you could travel she would go home. She always knew that. She just asked to have you here, and give you away, but I told her she could have time with you. I made the agreement because you could always go to her. She may not be in this time, but you can always go to see her," the goddess explained.

"Then teach me how to travel," I replied. I was getting bold, but I was desperate. I was sorely missing them by now.

"There were others before you," the goddess told me, not responding to my demand. "I have allowed many to be born that could travel and help others. I taught each one how to travel, and how to help bring people between times. Each person was good at heart and dedicated to helping mankind, or so I thought. One by one they turned. Each person became greedy. They would travel to make money. They would take the highest bidders. They never looked beyond their own pocketbooks. In turn, I had to destroy each stone I gave them. You are the last one I will allow to exist. You are the last chance. There are no stones left in this time beyond the ones left by the people who traveled here. Learning how to travel on your own will teach you to value what you were given, and hopefully make you different than the others."

The shimmery ghost-like figure of the goddess walked around to the side of the bed I was lying near. She was more translucent than the last time I saw her.

"I know you want your mother back, but she has a role to play in the past. It is where she is truly meant to be." The goddess's ghostly hand reached for mine.

"And you have a role to play, too. You will have to be strong, and follow your heart. I have no rules for you to follow as I had set for the ones before you. I know you will follow the path of right. I've already seen it. You are the one to save us from the darkness coming." The goddess let go of my hand and faded.

"Trust your heart, trust your friends, and remember to love," the goddess said before she was gone.

I sighed and blew my hair out of my face. Now that was really not making sense. If I thought she would give me more questions than answers, I wouldn't have called to her. No matter what she said about my mother, unless she was her happy in her own time, there was no way I could leave her there.

I looked back to my hand. The lines looked normal to me, or at least I thought they did. I tried again to go back to the library room. I had thought of Ty's shocked face and then I was instantly standing in the library and staring at it. I had a little vertigo and grabbed the table to keep from falling. I had just gone from lying on Seth's bed to standing before Ty. I sat down quickly, and Ty just watched me. I had done it. I traveled to the future and back, and I was still in one piece. Maybe the travel thing wasn't as hard as I imagined, or at least I hoped it wasn't.

"Okay that's just as creepy as appearing out of nowhere," Ty replied as I finally looked up from the table. "So?" Ty asked as I didn't speak.

Going from lying down to standing was a bit disorientating. I looked back to Ty's expectant face.

The door to the room burst open, and Sim spilled into the room, saving me from answering.

"There you two are," Sim said excitedly as her cheeks reddened. "Mari thought I imagined you coming back yesterday. I woke up this morning and you were gone. I had to think if you really were there or not. Then I heard your phone go off and knew you were back. It's been ringing non-stop since you left this morning"

I gave Sim a *"really, you want me to believe that"* look, and she smiled sweetly. She was the picture of a caring roomie.

"Okay, it's been going off since I woke and realized it was going off an hour ago," Sim replied. There was no way she was up all morning listening to it going off. "I figured someone calling that much must really need to talk to you."

She handed me my phone and turned to Ty.

"Did you have a good break?" Sim asked, her voice going a little higher. I had to smile as I opened my phone. I knew that voice was belonged to the Sim who had a crush on someone.

"Yeah, it was nice to be able to do nothing," Ty replied. Even he had a bit of a blush in his chocolate-colored cheeks. The new past was a bit more complicated than I remembered. I stood and took my phone outside the room. Sim and Ty were both great and deserved to be happy. If they made each other happy, then I would be happy, too.

Scrolling down to all my missed calls, I didn't even bother to listen to any of the messages. I turned my phone back off and peeked at Sim and Ty talking. There was no way I was responding to Logan. I was going to figure out the time travel stuff on my own.

4 CHAPTER

DEAL WITH THE DEVIL

The following weeks flew by. We returned from a week long break to only a week of classes, and then finals. I spent most of my time studying, and for once, everyone else did the same on campus. Well, except for Logan. He was more persistent than Seth was, and unfortunately, he knew me better than Seth did. When I was hiding in the library, Logan found me. When I took odd meal times, Logan was there. When I left class early, he was passing by. He never once spoke to me, but made sure that I knew he was still around, and his offer was still on the table. Even Sim noticed his silent advances.

"You really should just say yes to the boy," Sim told me one afternoon as we took a very late lunch. Logan, of course, was sitting across the room reading a book.

"No," I replied. There was no way I was saying yes to anything with Logan.

"And why not?" she asked, eyeing him over. "He's hot. He's nice. And he wants you bad."

I glanced at Logan. He caught my glance and smiled. My attention was going to be on my salad for the remainder of the meal. I couldn't exactly tell if he wanted me, or the favor he refused to name from me.

"I'd do anything to be pursued like that," Sim mused with dreamy eyes. I knew who she was talking about, but I knew he was nowhere near asking her out. When it came to girls, Ty was the shyest of the three guys from the past. He preferred to stay quietly in the shadow and observe everything.

"Then you can have Logan," I told Sim. "Because I'm not interested."

I stood up and threw my empty salad container away. I wasn't going to continue to sit around while Logan watched me from over his book. It was creepy, and it made me uncomfortable. He knew me too well. He was just one more distraction in my life. I had other things to worry about instead of Logan Jones.

The time traveling was getting easier, at least for traveling within a few days to the places I or Ty knew. I still had no clue about times further back or places I had never been. I was also hesitant to go too far into the past. We already knew that if I went back minutes, it would take hours to get enough power to come back. I was unsure how long I'd need to stay in the past before I'd be able to come back, and I was too afraid to try. And new places weren't working at all. We tried looking in books, looking online, anything visual, yet I still couldn't travel to them. The goddess said it would be easy, and it was for some and not for others. I didn't need the ability to go back days. I needed to go back centuries.

With break coming soon, we could work more on everything, but I felt like time was passing by too quickly. School took most of my time, and I needed to do well in my classes, but my mind was elsewhere. I had to keep reminding myself that I could go back at any time to get my mother. Just because a day passed here, it didn't mean it was a day in the past.

When the winter break finally arrived I was more than

happy to pack my car and make the long drive back to Chicago. While it would be more isolated to work at the Sangre home over break, I needed to be back with my grandfather. He was all alone now. Luckily, Ty didn't have any winter commitments with the team, so he was able to come back with me. I didn't ask what Logan was doing, but had the feeling if I was going to Chicago, so was he.

Ty and I got comfortable in my grandfather's house and soon began the same schedule we'd been doing at school between studying for finals: practice time travel in the morning, scour history books in the afternoon. We needed to know as much as we could before we went back. Ty couldn't remember where my mother was from since he wasn't as familiar with the area, but we had it narrowed down to three Middle Eastern cultures associated with the Egyptians: Hittite, Nahrin, and Assyrians. We studied each as we didn't know what to expect. After weeks of studying and travel practice, we were getting closer to our goal, but still not close enough. Now we were back in Chicago, and we were able to practice full-time.

"I think we should try with both of us tomorrow," Ty suggested as he paged through a book, sitting in my bedroom. He looked mainly at pictures.

"I don't know," I replied, not bothering to look up. I was actually reading my book.

"You said that yesterday, and the day before," Ty complained. He didn't like the study session part of our day.

"And I still don't know," I replied, unsure of everything. It was one thing to get myself stuck in some unknown time or place, but completely different to get Ty stuck there with me.

"You're just scared. It shouldn't be much different," Ty answered, shutting his book. Yes, it was break time for him.

He was right. I was scared. I was still scared each time I

did it. I wasn't sure where I'd end up, or if I would have to spend minutes or hours milling around wherever I went. I didn't want to be responsible for Ty, too. I didn't have control over traveling like I wanted, and I couldn't imagine throwing Ty in and then messing it up.

"Mari, I have faith in you. Now it's time that you do, too," Ty answered before standing up and leaving for dinner.

I smiled at Ty. He was what I needed right then; someone to believe in me. Seth had been the one to believe in us before, and now it was Ty. He truly was my best friend, and I was glad that hadn't changed with the past.

I mulled over what he said for the rest of the day. He was so sure we could do it. By the next morning I was as confident as Ty was that I could bring him back safely. He had no doubts, and therefore I had no doubts.

"If we just go back to yesterday, right after we left to drive here, it shouldn't be a problem," Ty said, turning his brown stone over in his hand as he talked. The stone flipped between his fingers. I was amazed by all the different colors of the chalcedony.

"Yes, yesterday," I replied. I reached out and took his hand. I pictured yesterday and felt the tingles begin. I used Ty's confidence and hurled us into the past day.

When the tingles stopped, I was in the living room of the Sangre beach home, alone. Nope, that didn't work. *So much for the confidence boost doing the job.* I shook my head and walked over to the couch, my new spot to sit and wait in defeat. It had been easy the past few days, and I thought it would be easy still. I didn't know what went wrong. We didn't try to go back too far. I looked at my arm. It wouldn't be more than thirty minutes before I could go back. We didn't go somewhere new. I had no idea what went wrong.

"Another visit from the future Mari?" Logan asked

from behind. I was getting used to his instant appearance. I looked up at him and was stopped by a thought. Was that it? Was he using his time travel to suddenly show up?

"What do you want, Logan?" I asked, though I really wanted to ask him if he was stalking me by traveling through time. Sim had bugged me since we got back from break about giving Logan the cold shoulder. She thought we made a perfect couple.

"I just want to help you," Logan replied. He sounded honest enough, but I still didn't buy it.

"Why?" I asked.

"Because you need it," Logan answered, smiling brightly at me. I couldn't refute that. We were getting nowhere, and this just proved it. "Just let me help you. I promise I won't ask that the favor to be something like asking you to leave Seth in the past."

I looked up at him and now analyzed him more. I hadn't thought that would be a favor request, but now I was even surer that I had to say *no* to him. If that was the first request he could think of that I wouldn't like, I hated to see what his other requests would be.

"Logan, I don't ever want to be anything with you other than friends, and even that's a stretch now. I get that you saved my past as much as you could." It really was nice that he did that, but it didn't change my gut feeling. "I have another goal beyond Seth at this point, but even so, I don't want a replacement."

"I never wanted to be a replacement," Logan replied, he tussled his dark blond hair, making me remember the boy I dated. "You and I once loved each other. That was built on a friendship. Why can't we just be friends now? Why can't I help you as a friend?"

"Friends don't ask for anything in return," I replied.

Logan grinned. "Touché."

I rolled my eyes. He was being so Logan. I was having a serious conversation, and I wasn't sure he was as serious.

He grinned more at my response. It was just what he was going for.

"Give me a chance. I can teach you how to do this in a matter of days, and then you can do as you please," Logan replied, holding out a hand to shake as a deal.

"No strings attached?" I asked. Logan paused and put a finger on his lips as he thought. He tapped his lips before smiling.

"How about I teach you for a kiss?" Logan suggested. "See, then there will be no leaving the boyfriend behind, or making you work off your debt doing devious deeds. Once I teach you everything you want to know about time travel, you just give me a little kiss." I was looking for the hidden intent. All he was asking was for a kiss.

"Really?" I asked. It wasn't like I hadn't kissed him hundreds of time in the past, but that seemed like a small payment compared to what I was imagining he'd ask for.

"Really," Logan replied, his violet eyes serious. "I'm not the evil, scheming monster you seem to think I am. I'm the guy you once loved and should remember quite well."

"Why?" I asked, still suspicious. With all the extra kisses Seth got from Melissa last fall, I wasn't going to feel bad kissing another guy at this point, but I was still missing something.

"I miss you," Logan replied. "The two years we were together were the best years of my life. I simply miss you. If teaching you how to time travel, even if it means you go back to your boyfriend, means I get to spend time with you, then I'll do that. I want our friendship back. You were the one I let get away. I know everything that happened was my fault. I'm sorry about it all. I want to make it up to you. Let me teach you," he pleaded. His eyes were filled with sincerity.

"Fine," I replied and stuck out my hand. Logan flashed his boyish grin and shook my hand.

"Deal then!"

"Now take me back home," I said to him, waving my hand around like an order. Ty already told me gatekeepers didn't work on the same goddess magic, and could travel as they pleased. If Logan was going to help me, he could start by making me stay less in the past.

Logan smiled more and offered me his arm. I looped mine in his like we were going for a walk. Instantly we were back in my room, and Ty was beside me. Ty took a step back at my sudden appearance with Logan.

"Logan is going to teach us how to time travel," I told Ty before he could even ask. "Obviously traveling with someone isn't as easy as we thought it would be."

"First lesson starts tomorrow," Logan said, nodding to me and then Ty. With a wink he was gone.

"Is that such a good idea?" Ty asked.

I shrugged. The Logan I knew was hidden somewhere inside the man that was now my new teacher. *A good idea?* No. It was possible that he still had other motives for teaching me. I'd know soon enough. He could either be helping me out of the goodness of his heart, or I had a made a deal with the devil. I hoped it wasn't the latter or I was screwed.

Logan came over the next day bright and early, and when I say early, I mean it was even early for me. I had just woken up and made it downstairs to grab some breakfast, and he was sitting in the living room, waiting. He was chatting away with my grandfather when I finally came in the room.

"Good morning, Mari," my grandfather said as I gave him a kiss on the cheek. He was still frailer than I ever remembered, but he had gained most of the bounce back in his voice after my mother left us. He was recovering from the shock of her loss better than I was.

"Good morning, Grandfather," I replied.

"Do I get one, too?" Logan asked, tapping his own cheek. My grandfather chuckled. Logan had been winning over my grandfather again. I'd say my grandfather was probably the most devastated of everyone when I dumped Logan. He tried, for weeks, to get me to talk to Logan again.

"Regretting letting her go now?" my grandfather asked Logan in a teasing manner. Grandfather always thought Logan was to blame for not trying harder to win me back.

"Every single day," Logan replied in all seriousness.

"I'll go wake up Ty," I told both of them. I didn't invite Logan to come with me. His seriousness still made me worry about our agreement. He wasn't going to win me back. I had moved on.

As I approached Ty's door, it opened. He was an early riser, too. I wasn't used to that after a semester with Sim. I could never figure out how one person could sleep as late as she could, but she was just as baffled by me.

"Our teacher is here," I said, pointing down the hallway.

Ty nodded. "Are you sure we can trust him?"

"The Logan I knew two years ago, I'd say yes to trusting," I replied. "This Logan?" I shrugged. I wasn't sure, but I didn't have many more options.

"But didn't you break up with him because he was never around, and running off all the time?" Ty asked. "Will he really make a good teacher?"

"Which now makes more sense since he was doing a job the whole time. I have a feeling he wasn't cheating on me like I thought, just cheating on me with his time traveling side-job. Do I trust him now? Not completely. But what else can we do? We've been working at this for weeks and still can't go back far enough into the past, and after yesterday I learned that I can't take you. In order for us to go back and get my mother, we need to be able to do both," I explained. Ty nodded. We both had some distrust of Logan, but we didn't have a choice now. We needed his help. At least we were going into the situation with our eyes open.

We returned to the living room, and Logan was waiting alone. He stood as we entered.

"We probably want to go someplace quieter. A bedroom or somewhere," Logan suggested, "where we won't be interrupted." I got the hint at what he was suggesting. I wasn't inviting him to my room. That was too weird.

"We can go back to my room," Ty recommended, like the over-protective brother he was becoming to me.

"Sounds good," Logan replied, not missing a beat.

We followed Ty back to his surprisingly clean room. I sat down in the desk chair to avoid sitting anywhere near Logan. His choices were chairs across the room or the bed. Ty caught my move and stood over near me to further discourage Logan from coming close.

"I've seen you've worked out the beginnings of travel, but what more do you want to learn how to do?" Logan asked as he chose a chair.

"I need to learn how to travel further into the past. My best is three days, right?" I asked Ty for confirmation. He nodded in agreement. "I need to learn how to go somewhere I haven't been before. I've only gone to locations I have been to, and most of them were places I've been recently."

"That's not a problem," Logan replied.

"And I need to learn how to take people with me," I added. That was the most important part. I wouldn't be rescuing anyone if I couldn't take them with me.

"That might be more work," Logan replied. "Your carnelian is only for your travel, not another person."

"We have stones," I answered back. "Ty has his that he uses to travel." I didn't know why I didn't tell him about the chrysoprase stone, but that much needed to stay a secret.

"You do?" Logan asked, sitting up a bit. I guess we had surprised him.

"How else do you think Ty got here?" I replied.

"Yeah, that makes sense," Logan replied, hiding his surprise a bit. "Well, in that case, all three problems are really not a problem."

"You can teach me how to do all that?" I asked suspiciously. He had agreed easily.

"Yeah, maybe by the time break is done we can have you able to travel anywhere," Logan replied.

"By the time break is done?" I asked, disappointed. Break was going to be five more weeks.

"Yes. Taking someone with you or going somewhere new aren't very hard to do. But the travel into the past will take time. You'll need days between trips to recover the goddess stone's power," Logan explained.

That actually made sense, but I just didn't like how long it would take. At least he wasn't trying to drag out the learning. Logan didn't seem to mind the length of training in the least, but I did. I hated that I already had to go too long without my mom and Seth.

"Then what do we start with?" I asked, ready to begin.

"How about going somewhere new?" Logan replied. Of course he'd pick the one not including Ty.

"Like where?" I asked.

"I know this place in Tahiti. It's a little beach place. They serve the best drinks," Logan replied. Yes, exactly what I wanted to do: go drinking with my ex-boyfriend.

"Umm, isn't it best to go somewhere without a lot of people?" I answered to avoid saying no outright.

"I suppose," Logan replied, pressing his fingers together in thought. "You are quite new at this." Logan thought for a moment. "We should go to Molokini. It's a bird sanctuary in Hawaii. I'm sure we won't find anyone there. It's illegal for people to go onto the island, even though they snorkel around it."

"Okay," I replied. That didn't help me much. He still hadn't explained how to do it to me. I waited patiently as Logan stared at me.

"Are you not even going to try?" Logan asked.

"I already know I can't go anywhere new. I've tried many times," I replied and heard Ty chuckle. There was nothing to try. I didn't even know what Molokini looked like.

"Really?" Logan asked, like I wasn't telling the truth. I rolled my eyes at him and Ty laughed more.

"Really," I responded. I remembered the many tries and the laughs Ty gave me each time. The last time he thought I was going to burst a vein in my head from staring so hard at the picture of where I was trying to go.

"Okay, fine," Logan added. "Close your eyes," he directed. I stole a glance at Ty, and he smiled back. My trust in Logan was going to have to start now. I just hoped I wasn't wrong, and that the old Logan was somewhere still inside him.

"Closed," I replied, when I had finally closed them. "Now what?"

"Impatient?" Logan asked.

"Um, yes, you said this would take weeks to learn, so I have to get going on it." I peeked at him through my eyelashes. He put his hand over my eyes when he caught my peek and my eyes automatically closed again.

"Think of a large map, maybe a globe would help," Logan said.

I did just that. I thought of a globe, covered in blue and green.

"Find Hawaii. It is out in the Pacific Ocean," Logan added. I would have rolled my eyes at him if I could. I knew where Hawaii was. "Now look closely at those islands. One is labeled now. Find it."

He was right. As I got closer to the globe to look at the small islands that made up Hawaii, there was a crescent-shaped one labeled Molokini. He had to be putting those images in my head, and I never had heard of the island before.

"How?" I asked.

"Your knowledge is already in your head how to travel; you just need to learn how. One last thing as you look at the map. Get closer to our destination and look at the ground. We don't want to end up tumbling down a hill, or in the water. Look at the very peak of the crescent and the ground in that area. Imagine yourself sitting there," Logan gave his last advice before I felt the tingles.

Upon closer inspection, this island wasn't much of an island. There were no beaches, and the lack of greenery was surprising. I found the ridge that Logan described and imagined sitting on it. Without pausing to think any more, I was actually sitting there. Birds cawed at the start of a new day. In the dawn sky in Hawaii, I was sitting on an uninhabited island that was off-limits to people. I was breaking the law just for being there. Then, instantly, I was back at home. Logan flashed right behind me.

"You didn't want to stay and see the sun rise?" Logan asked. "It really is beautiful from that island. Nothing to stop the view."

"How did I do that?" I asked.

"Um, I thought I was pretty good with my directions," Logan replied.

I shook my head. I wasn't unsure about how we got there. "No. I mean come right home," I replied, walking over and joining Ty on the bed. The tips of the lines on my arms were a little faded, yet still there. Ty was looking over my arm, too.

"When you jump in current time it shouldn't use much

of the stone up, allowing you to make several jumps before you can't again. And when you jump in a controlled manner, it uses even less. What you have been doing thus far has been all instinct. Your jumps were never controlled, and the stone used up greatly. Now you're controlling it. It shouldn't use as much power to go back and forth," Logan added, moving over to stand before me. He took my hand and looked at the lines.

"I'd guess we have enough time to eat and move on to the next lesson," Logan assessed.

"Next lesson?" I asked. Ty and I had only been practicing jumping through time once a day.

"Yeah, why not? You seem to be in a hurry," Logan replied, leading the way to the door. Ty and I followed. I guess he was more serious about teaching me than I thought he'd be.

I was surprised he was being so helpful. At breakfast he was busy talking about all his travels, telling Ty about one adventure after another. He had been to almost any imaginable time in the past or the future. He had seen things and knew things that were only in history books. Logan was only my age, but by the way he talked, he had lived at least three lifetimes by now. He easily joked with Ty, and he seemed to be as normal as I remembered. He could always charm anyone he met. By the time breakfast was done the carnelian lines were back to normal.

We went back to Ty's room, and I waited for my next lesson. I was getting closer to my mother with each step and more anxious to see Seth again. Logan made it all out to be much easier than I had imagined. I still didn't understand why the goddess didn't help me. I was hoping each lesson would be as easy, but I had a feeling that would not be the case.

"If we do travel with someone else in the present time, we should be able to do one more this afternoon," Logan replied as he stepped into the room. "I'm assuming you want to take Ty with you somewhere, and since he has a stone, it should be fine. Why don't we just take Ty over to my house? You always seemed to like the library."

Ty raised his eyebrows at me. Yes, Logan knew a lot about me. Ty already knew that I dated Logan for two years. I guess Logan's remembrance of me was a bit much for even Ty after all the lunch tales. Logan didn't seem to forget a detail, especially when it was about me. He could place each time he went missing on me while we were dating. I was sure now that he wasn't cheating with another girl, just his job.

"Ty, you have your stone?" Logan said to Ty. Ty stood and opened his bag on one of the chairs in the room. He pulled out the brown stone he always had somewhere with him. Logan nodded to him. "Mari, take his hand with the stone between you. You should be able to feel the stone. Feel the power in the stone. When you find your location, make sure you remember to visualize him there beside you. If not, you might just leave him behind."

"Again," Ty added, under his breath. I smacked him, but that was a stupid idea. Ty was all muscle in his upper body and my hand hurt afterward. Ty just laughed at my attempt. I couldn't help but want to stick my tongue out at him.

"Mari, concentrate," Logan said to me as he gently pulled my face forward from responding to Ty again. His hands were soft. For someone who traveled around the world to all these unique locations, and went on all sorts of adventures, you'd expect him to at least have hands that were a little rougher.

"Where to again, boss?" I asked once I was over my distraction of Ty.

"My house, the library. No one should be working right now, so you don't have to worry about seeing anyone like you would here. If you went to your own library, you'd probably scare your own grandfather into a heart attack," Logan replied, still holding my face to make sure I was listening to him.

I nodded, breaking his hold and closing my eyes. I saw the Jones house and the library. My body started to fuzz and the feeling was strongest at my hand where I was connected to Ty. It would be funny to pop into my own library, but Logan was right that it would scare my grandfather. As soon as we faded, I regretted my last thought. I didn't need to open my eyes to know what I did. We were exactly where I was told not to be, my own library and not the Jones'. Luckily, Ty was beside me and my grandfather wasn't around.

Ty began laughing.

"What?" I asked. "I didn't really mean to take us here."

"I wasn't laughing at the location. I was laughing because you did it. I had no clue how we'd figure out this time travel thing, but I guess making a deal with Logan was the right thing to do after all," Ty replied as he stopped his laugh. "Once we save your mother, we can go back to be with Seth and his family. We won't need to save them or bring them back. We can just stay there."

"But why would you want to go back?" I asked. I had always thought I'd bring the guys back to the present. I hadn't considered going back to be with them. "There isn't a life there for you. You're a slave to his family. Wouldn't you like to just stay here?"

"I'm a slave there for now. But my father promised me that once I was a man, he'd come for me. My father is the leader of our people. I just became a man back home, and after we returned from the campaign I know my father will come. I will be going home," Ty explained. His eyes were twinkling at the thought.

I smiled at him. It was no choice. After we saved my mom, we would go back to the past to live. Seth had already made a way for me to stay with him that I could agree to. It only seemed right to return Ty. I always thought he was a slave for life, but it seemed it was more of an indentured servant. He talked about his family he missed, and I thought that would be why he wanted to go back. He couldn't wait to get home to them. My list just continued to grow. I had to save my mom. I had to save Ty. And I wanted to be with Seth. We still had weeks of training before we could attempt to go back. Hopefully, my list wouldn't grow any more.

"Should we go off to the right library this time?" I asked, holding out my hand.

Ty placed his hand in mine and grinned. "Sure thing, Miss Time-Traveler. Let's go see where the devil lives."

"Ty," I complained. "You were just saying it was good we were getting help from him."

"It doesn't make him any less devious. I see the way he looks at you. Sure, he may be helping us, but that doesn't mean he doesn't have his own plan, and I know it involves you. He looks at you the same way that Seth does," Ty explained. I hated to hear that. No matter how many times I told Logan I didn't want to be with him, it didn't seem to sink in at all.

"There is nothing to worry about. Logan knows I don't want a boyfriend. He knows I want to be with Seth," I answered. I hope that much at least.

"But that doesn't mean he doesn't want to be with you," Ty replied.

I shook my head. I actually felt less like Logan was trying to persuade me since we made the agreement. I hadn't caught him staring at me once like I had all the time when we were at school. Logan was being nicer and much more friendly now, not a hint of suggestiveness that we should get together. Well, at least not more than the normal Logan would be. Ty had to be wrong.

"No distractions," I told him as I took his hand again and concentrated.

"Yes, boss," Ty replied, pretending to salute with his

free hand.

I was going to do it right this time. I pictured the Jones house library, and the book that called to me at the party over Thanksgiving. By the time I finished thinking of the book we were there, standing in front of it. Ty took a breath and moved a few feet away from me.

"I've never done that more than a once in a day. That was a bit weird," Ty commented, shaking out the hand that had been touching the stone.

I nodded and looked down at the book with the ancient text. I still felt a hum coming off the book. I wanted to touch it and see if the pages were humming like I felt they would be. I peered into the box and looked at the weird lines. It was nothing I could understand. I looked up and around the room. Logan wasn't there. I really wanted to touch the book.

"What is it?" Ty asked, stepping behind me and looking over my shoulder.

"I don't know. Something about the book makes me feel like I should touch it. Like if I touched it I would know the secret it's trying to tell me," I explained. "Gosh, that sounds weird," I added as I turned around.

"Weird? Yes. But I've seen a lot of weird things happen since we first found these stones," Ty said, holding his up. The glow I normally saw off the stone was gone. I looked down to my arm. The lines were faded around the edges. We were going to have to wait until the power returned, or for Logan.

I looked up at Ty. I really wanted to see why I should touch the book. Ty nodded to me. It didn't matter how weird it was, I was going to try. I looked around the room one more time. Ty stayed right behind me, he was so big that if anyone was in the room they would be blocked from actually seeing me while I touched the book. It felt like I was stealing, or doing something wrong. These texts were old and priceless. Oils from your hands could damage the paper, but I still had to know. The longer I stood there, the more the book pulled at me. I lifted the glass case only enough to get a finger in to touch the text. I slid my finger in and felt the shock as I touched it. I quickly pulled my hand out in surprise.

I turned back to Ty to tell him what happened when the shimmer of Logan traveling into the room caught my eye.

"There you are," Logan said, like he had been searching for us.

"I saw you leave your house, and when I came here, you weren't anywhere to be found. I looked around the house first in case you ended up in a different room, and then went back to your place. What happened?" Logan asked, brushing Ty aside and looking me over, like I could get hurt from the time traveling. Once he was satisfied I was okay, he backed up and waited for an answer.

"I got distracted at the last moment when we left. We ended up in my grandfather's library, not this one. Once we realized that, we came here. But we can't go anywhere else." I held up my arm. The lines were growing again, but they still weren't fully to where they should be.

"That was much better than what I was picturing," Logan admitted. "I knew you were a natural at this time travel thing, but I was still worried. I think I prefer that you practice taking me places from now on, at least until you get the hang of it."

Ty raised his eyebrows at me from his position beside Logan. Logan couldn't see it, but since I was facing both of them, I could. There was nothing about Logan's worry that made me feel like he was interested in me. We had decided to be friends. I would be just as worried about Sim if I were teaching her time traveling and lost her.

"Do we stay here or go back to Mari's place?" Ty asked, changing the subject.

"We can go back to Mari's house so that her

grandfather doesn't get worried," Logan replied. "I'll take you both back. I can only take one person at a time."

"I'll go first," Ty suggested, probably trying not to get left behind.

Logan placed a hand on his shoulder and was gone without a goodbye. I turned around and looked at the book. It didn't hum for me anymore after getting zapped, but I was surprised that I could read the text. I skimmed over a little bit before the tingle of someone coming distracted me. That was new. I could feel Logan coming back, and I could read an ancient text that had just been illegible.

Logan was standing where he left. He walked a few steps to be right in front of me. He looked me over again. I had no clue what he was searching for.

"Are you sure you're okay?" Logan asked. He was really concerned. "Maybe we should put off this afternoon's lessons."

"Logan, I'm fine," I replied, looking down at myself. Why would anything be wrong?

"I should have been more careful," Logan answered back. He was still overly concerned. "Maybe we should just practice more by going to a location you want to go to."

"Logan. I.AM. FINE." I pushed his chin up so that he looked me in the eyes as I repeated it again, slower for him.

"I know," Logan said quieter. "But if something happened, I'd feel bad. I shouldn't assume you can do all this when your first travel was only less than a month ago. I keep forgetting she didn't teach you."

"Why are you worried?" I asked.

"It is dangerous to time travel, Mari. You should already be aware of that. I just worry that you might end up somewhere you don't intend to be," Logan replied, holding out a hand for me to take. "The world is not always a forgiving place to be in any time period."

I took his hand and was instantly in my own bedroom.

"You should get some rest," Logan said, pointing to my bed. "Time travel can be draining when you're doing the work. I'll be back later this evening for another lesson."

Logan gave me another once over and then disappeared. Ty stood in the open doorway.

"I figured he'd take you back to your own room," Ty replied as I looked to him. "Why is he worried?" Ty asked.

"I have no clue," I replied. I really didn't. Yes, time travel was dangerous, but I could already travel within days without a problem. And if he was worried we went somewhere dangerous, I had Ty with me. Just his size alone was imposing.

"Do you need some rest?" Ty asked.

"Actually, I think I do, and I don't think it has to do with time travel," I replied. "That book. I think touching it gave me the ability to read it, and my mind is on an overload right now."

"See, not too weird that a book called to you. It just wanted to be read." Ty winked at me and walked away. "I'll keep reading, or rather looking at pictures," he called from down the hallway.

Logan returned that evening, but he was a bit hesitant to teach me anything. He wanted to wait to teach me more, but I still didn't see the danger he was worried about. I had a moment of distraction, and I was sure not to repeat that again. I didn't want to end up in some rainforest with giant bugs somewhere. Logan had to know I was serious, but he seemed too worried to notice.

"I need to practice all you taught me, but I still need to learn how to travel back in time further than a few days," I told Logan to remind him why he was even stopping by.

Logan nodded. "We can do that, but I'm holding onto you from now on. I'm not letting you run off alone." Surprisingly, Ty seemed to like that idea. It must have been his protective side winning over his teasing side at that point.

"How about we try two weeks?" Logan suggested.

"I have no idea what I was doing two weeks ago exactly," I replied. He had just picked an arbitrary time.

"I meant two weeks ago somewhere else. I think two weeks ago in Key West would be nice. We could arrive right at sunset. The tourists go to the pier on one side of the island to view the sunset. There's an old fort on the other side of the island that closes at that time. Most people clear out before, so it should be fairly empty," Logan explained what had appeared to be a random choice.

"Okay. How we do this, then?" I asked.

Logan walked over and took my hand in his. It had been two years, yet his touch was all too familiar. The concern Logan was showing was closer to how I remembered him, and I was having a hard time keeping in mind that he wasn't the same now. His hand was warm, and his touch was still familiar. My heartbeat increased a little, like the first time he took my hand in his. I closed my eyes, waiting for him to give me directions, and to allow myself to calm down. I didn't like Logan any more. He was not the same. He was different. I liked Seth.

"Okay, we need to do the map again. You need to picture where to go. Think of Florida and the islands that jet off the bottom of the state. Follow those islands to the last one in the chain," Logan explained, unaware, thankfully, of my heart beating faster. I forgot about my heart and listened to him. I had to concentrate. "Go to that last island and look closer. On the north side of the island you will see lots of people. Head to the south, to the point that jets out into the ocean on the southeast side of the island."

I followed exactly what he explained. I could see that the north side was filled with tiny little people. They stood around groups of performers. I let the map move and went south like he directed me, toward the south. Pedestrians strolled through the street. We passed over a black-topped lighthouse. I reached the water and moved east. Soon I was hovering over a large stone fort. It looked old. South of it was a bunch of trees and a beach. I found where we wanted to go, but I was pretty sure it was in present time.

"Now that you are there," Logan continued as if he saw the same thing as me. Who knew? Maybe he could, since I was still holding his hand. "Look at the fort. It has four little pieces jetting out. Find one of those and focus there. That's where we will end up. Please don't put us in the moat. Now, concentrate on that one spot and will time to change, feel it rewind the two weeks you want."

I looked at one of the points on the fort and waited. Two people still stood around until a park ranger ushered them away. Sure enough, the scene changed. It grew brighter and then darker as night set in and day came back. Time picked up and flew by. It became a colorful whirl. Suddenly it stopped. It was still dusk, but now there were no people standing around, and no ranger ushering them away. Soon my body began to fade and reappear exactly where I was looking.

Logan was beside me, holding tight to my hand. He looked around, surprised. The sun was almost set and casting a pretty purple glow across the sky. I felt the magic of being there and being able to just jump anywhere in time. Happiness tingled in me from head to toe. I was different. I could travel through time. I could see the world. This was magical.

Logan held my hand more gently as all my realizations set in. The world was not as scary as it once was. I was afraid college was the last time I could get to be me. I'd have to join my grandfather in his business, and live out my life never having really lived it. Now I didn't have to worry about that. I could live life and have any adventure I wanted. I had the power to go through time and be anywhere in the world in the blink of an eye. It was amazing to feel the power within me. My life had just changed completely. I wasn't afraid anymore. I was in control.

"Magical," I said quietly as the last rays set. It was a perfect sixty-five degrees even though we had just left snow.

"It sure is," Logan replied. I didn't turn to look at him, but I sensed he wasn't staring at the sunset.

Logan pulled me over to the edge of the fort we stood by and up on the top of the fort roof that had warning signs.

"Um, we're not supposed to climb on this," I replied, pointing to the signs.

Logan gave me boyish grin that told me he didn't care. I still didn't move. "The rangers won't look for us. We didn't enter the park from their point of view. Once they have their head count correct, they closed up. Trust me. No one will know."

"What if it's dangerous?" I asked. I wasn't afraid of heights, but climbing on a slightly crumbling structure never seemed like a good idea.

"Then don't let go of my hand. If anything happens, I'll just send us home," Logan replied.

"Why don't we head home now?" I asked.

"Because I want you to try going forward, too. And I know you'll need time to re-energize," Logan replied, squeezing my carnelian hand to remind me. "Come on. We can sit and watch the stars a bit. It is a beautiful night, not a cloud in the sky. I'd say we're safe to sit here a little bit."

I let him lead me forward. We climbed up past the warning signs. They were there for a reason, but I guess we didn't need to follow rules. I held tight to his hand. I didn't know if I could get myself home if I got in trouble. I basically had no choice. We sat down on a ledge, and the sky darkened. Nighttime was completely upon us now. The park was silent, and all you heard was the water and occasional wildlife. It was actually quite peaceful.

"Mari, have you ever wondered if I had told you the truth about who I was, would you still be with me?" Logan asked.

I was startled by the question. I hadn't thought of that.

"I mean," Logan added, seeing my hesitation. "We were quite good together, if you ask me. We never fought beyond me leaving for work. I was always happy, and I thought you were, too. We had so much fun. Remember that time that we convinced Amy that they were making space trips to the moon?"

That was kind of funny. She didn't spend any of her allowance for two weeks as she thought she would get a seat on the moon plane we told her about. I smiled. Yes, we had fun times, but I remembered the rough times, too, like when he would leave me alone somewhere, and I'd be left waiting for him to return, if he ever did. There were many times I drove myself home in his car. He always came back apologizing and bringing me a gift, and I always forgave him. That was the problem with our relationship to begin with. I always forgave him, therefore he never changed. I slid my hand from his. It wasn't completely safe, but I feared I was giving him the wrong idea. I'd be safe where we were sitting if I didn't move.

"I never once meant to hurt you," Logan said gently. I turned to look at him and felt the stones beneath me wobble a bit. Logan slid his arm around my waist to keep me on the edge and from slipping away.

"But you did," I replied. Tears began to well up in my

eyes. I had cried enough over Logan Jones, but now everything came right back to how I felt two years ago. "Again and again. I told you it hurt, and you promised to never do it again. Yet, you always did."

"And I will regret that for the rest of my life. I'm sorry about everything, especially prom. I'm hoping in some form I can make it up to you. I miss you. I miss your smile. I miss your humor. I miss your kisses." Logan used his free hand to brush hair out of my face. "I'll do anything to win you back. And if that isn't possible, I'll do anything to make you happy."

My heart beat harder in my chest. I waited two years to hear him say those words. Two long years of not looking for someone else. Two long years of not trusting any guy. Logan had turned my life upside down when I dumped him. And now he was finally telling me he was sorry. But it was too late. I had moved on.

"Then help me find Seth. I love him, and he makes me happy. If you truly want me to be happy, help me," I replied, turning around to get off the unstable wall where I was forced to touch him and remember a past that was completely different now that I knew the truth. "All I can be with you is friends."

"Have you ever thought of what Seth might be doing in the past?" Logan asked. There was no malice or hate, it was just a simple question. Yes, I had thought about it, and often wondered. "He doesn't live in a time where he can wait around years until you come back. His father had already made an arrangement for him before he brought you back. He will be expected to marry and carry on his lineage. He will be expected to love and have children with someone else. You are not of his time. He can't sit around waiting for you."

Logan said exactly what I had been thinking. All the bad what ifs I had ever questioned were coming out of his mouth. If I didn't go back to the exactly the right time,

Seth would have moved on. He would be with someone else, and I would have been forgotten.

"He wouldn't do that to me," I replied. I had to believe that Seth loved me as much as I loved him. There was no way I could just move on without Seth, and I hoped he couldn't without me.

"He wouldn't have a choice," Logan replied. That was true. I had met Seth's dad, the general. I doubt he ever gave Seth a choice in anything. "What will you do if you go back and he's married? Will you ruin the life he built without you?" That was a question I didn't want to answer.

I felt tears welling up. I didn't want to think about that. I didn't want Seth to move on, but I had no control if he did or not. I was spending all my time trying to get back to him, but he could already not be there waiting for me. I hated that thought, and it killed me inside. I hoped that I could find him in the past and he would be waiting for me, but there was a good chance he wouldn't be. His life was there and not here.

"I will never hurt you again," Logan said. "I promise you that, Mari. If you let me be the one, I will give you anything you want. I can make you happy. Seth will only bring you sadness. He isn't from our time. I love you, Mari, and I know you can love me, too, if you tried. The spark between us isn't gone. It can never be gone."

I scooted down past the warning sign and to the solid ground. Distance was needed. It was too confusing to be close to him. I didn't feel the constant flutters in my stomach when I was around Logan like I did with Seth, yet his touch still made my heart beat faster. He was my first love. I had heard you never truly got over your first love, but this was harder than I thought. He was saying everything I needed to hear. It was easy to be over him when I thought he was a jerk, but now it wasn't as easy.

Logan followed me.

"After traveling so much today, you should probably not do anything tomorrow. You will be tired. It takes time to get used to, and the further you go back, the more you have to recover," Logan explained, going back to teacher mode.

"Sure. I'll relax tomorrow," I replied.

Logan stopped right behind me. I could feel his breath on my head. I didn't know how much more I could be around him. He was making me think too much. What would have happened two years ago if I knew the truth? Would we still be together? Would I have forgiving him for running away time and time again? Would I have ever met Seth? I shook my head to stop the questions. The reality was that I did meet Seth, and I did find that someone could make me happier than Logan ever had. I needed space from Logan. He confused me with everything he said.

"I think I have all the basics down now. Maybe I won't need you to come back and oversee my practice," I told him as I turned. Logan had stopped only inches from me. I was staring at his chest. If I looked up our lips would only be inches apart. That wasn't a good place to be if I wanted to convince him that all I wanted to be was friends. I moved to step back, and he caught me by wrapping his arms around my waist.

"Is that what you truly want?" Logan asked, his deep violet eyes staring hard at me. My hands rested on his chest, and I was frozen although I wanted to push him away. It was way too familiar.

"It's what I want," I replied, even though I wasn't completely sure now with his arms around me. It felt too real. Too much like a life that I remembered also enjoying.

"Then you owe me my payment," he said huskily, waiting for what he wanted, and I now just figured out it was a very bad deal to have made.

But a deal was a deal. I stood up on my tippy-toes and moved to kiss his cheek. I never agreed the kiss had to be on the lips. Logan turned his head and caught my lips with his own. Too many memories came flooding back at once. I remembered those lips, and I remembered those kisses that always made me weak in the knees. My hands decided, on their own, to wrap around his neck and pull him closer. His lips brought back feelings I had forgotten. He deepened the kiss at my response and pulled me tighter, pressing my body to his. He wasn't the only one who still remembered everything. Memories kept rolling through my mind. The kiss, his lips against mine, was everything I had pictured as my goodbye kiss I never got to give him when I cut him out of my life cold turkey. I moved on. I went to pull away, but by now his hands were tangled in my hair and mine in his. I panicked and thought of home where we left Ty standing.

The shock of shifting through time brought Logan back to reality as he slid his hands down around my waist, yet he refused to end the kiss. It became even more of a reality when we appeared before Ty.

Ty took one look at us with my hands on Logan's chest and Logan holding me tight against him with our lips still together. Ty pulled me from Logan and with all one motion punched Logan in the face. Logan stumbled back and wiped the blood dripping down his nose.

"How dare you touch her?" Ty said, getting ready to punch Logan again.

"We'll have to do that again," Logan said teasingly to me as Ty fumed. Logan looked to Ty for only an instant before beginning to fade away. As I caught my last glimpse of Logan, he winked at me and smiled. He still wasn't giving up on me.

I was more confused than ever. I still had some hidden feelings left for him that I didn't want to have. Maybe he did just want to help me, maybe he had other plans. One

B KRISTIN McMICHAEL

thing was for sure- I didn't want to be alone with Logan any more. There was too much left between us, even though I had moved on. Logan wasn't used to taking no for an answer, and I had a feeling that he was going to always be around somehow. My life needed to be Logan-free.

92

CHAPTER 5

GETTING ANSWERS

Ty and I spent the next two weeks working on the time travel practice. We would pick the locations and times, and I would travel there. I was getting better at visualizing the map and going places faster. I was getting better at feeling the power of the goddess stone when Ty held it so that I didn't need to be touching it at the same time. Slowly we also discovered that I could push Ty through time back to my room. I didn't even want to try somewhere else, but that was enough to know that if we encountered trouble, I could get him home if needed. As Logan predicted, it was slow going. We had to wait days in between any lengthy travel and had to be careful to pick locations that I could hide in for hours when I went places.

The weeks passed quickly and before long it was already the holidays. Ty had to return to the Sangre house in Chicago which turned out to be Logan's house, and we were invited to attend dinner there for the holidays. I really didn't want to attend, but my grandfather looked a bit down without my mother around. I did my best to keep his spirits up, and I had to be there with him as his date. I could do it for my grandfather, but nobody said I would have to talk to Logan. I could ignore him, but I had to be polite since it was Mr. Sangre that invited us.

The ride over to the Sangre house was quiet, and I didn't attempt to fill the silence. My mind was reeling with too many thoughts to have an actual conversation. Ty had been at the Sangre house for two days now, and I was ready to get back to traveling. We had been planning a trip the furthest back we thought we could travel safely. We planned to go back to Ty's village before he left it. He knew his way around, and he could keep us hidden and safe while we waited to return. It would tell us if we were ready to try getting my mom back home.

When we reached the house, my grandfather finally spoke.

"We only have to stay for the dinner," my grandfather told me. He might have noticed that Logan was no longer around.

"What?" I asked. I was expecting to have to stay hours while the older men all talked. At least I had Ty and would be entertained by him, I hoped.

"I know something happened again with you and Logan. I don't want you to have to stay here any longer than you're comfortable with," my grandfather added. "I may be old, but I'm not blind."

While I was off in my own world trying to get my mom back, I had forgotten how observant my grandfather was. He was paid for his attention to detail, so that was to be expected.

"I want to stay for you," I replied, reaching over and taking his hand. I wanted him to be happy during the holidays. "Ty will be here. Talk and visit as long as you'd like. I'm sure the two of us can find something to do that won't get us into trouble." I grinned at him and he smiled back.

"You look too much like her," he said as he stared at me.

"Well, I hope so. She is my mother after all," I replied. "Please, Grandfather, don't worry about me. I will be fine with Ty. We're friends."

"And that worries me, too," my grandfather added. "I know you two are up to something. You are always talking for hours and reading away at those history books in the library. I can guess it has something to do with finding your mother. Yes, at first I wanted your mother back, but now I have grown to accept it. I was given twenty years with her as my daughter. She filled a void in my heart I didn't even know I had. But now it's time to let her have her life. She never did have a life here. She always was with me, taking care of me. I want her to be happy, and if that's in the past, then that is where she belongs."

"And what if she isn't happy?" I asked. It was my major concern.

"Then she will find a way to come back. You don't need to risk everything to find her. You can stay here and grow up like she wanted. You can have a life here," he replied as the car pulled up in front of the house. Our chauffeur came out and opened my door.

"I can't leave her in the past if she isn't happy," I said before exiting the car. I waited for him to stand out of the car. And I couldn't have a life without Seth.

"You get that from her, you know. She was just as stubborn," he told me. He offered me his arm, and I took it. "Now, no more talk of dabbling in things you should let go. Let's go spread some holiday cheer." His voice actually sounded hopeful. Maybe he really was moving on.

Mr. Sangre and Logan greeted us at the doorway. When Logan bent down to kiss my cheek I tried not to blush. It was too weird after how I last saw him. While Mr. Sangre chatted with my grandfather, I stood and looked around the house. I wasn't about to chat with Logan.

"Mari," Ty boomed, coming up to the doorway and

taking me away from the Sangres.

"Lifesaver," I whispered to him.

"Always," he replied. He led me away from the dining room. "Dinner won't be ready yet for at least another twenty minutes," he explained. He kept us walking away. There were several more rooms in the direction we were walking, but I had no clue where we were going now. By the time Ty finally stopped to open the door, he was leading me outside by the pool.

"It's a little chilly to be going for a swim," I commented.

"Not a swim. We need to get to my room for a little light reading," he replied cryptically.

Ty led us past the pool, and I regretted giving my coat away inside. Luckily it wasn't far, and he was opening a door to the pool house. Once inside, he shut the door behind me and locked it. It was warmer in here and the slight chill I had from our walk around the pool was gone instantly.

"You know that doesn't exactly keep any of the Sangre family out," I said to him.

"Actually, I think it does," Ty replied. "I locked it the first day I came here, and Logan had to pound on the door to wake me. I have no idea why, but I don't think you can time travel into this room." That was an interesting idea.

"Can you travel out?" I asked.

"I dunno. Try it," Ty suggested.

I pictured the area outside the door. I was just looking at it moment ago. It wouldn't take much to go back there. I could just appear there and walk back in. Well, once Ty unlocked the door. But, strangely, nothing happened. I was still inside. I thought again and waited. It should have been instant. It wasn't.

"Guess not," Ty said before I could.

"There must be places you can't time travel from," I observed. That had never crossed my mind. I had to be a bit more careful now. I really didn't want to get stuck somewhere.

"That was the first interesting thing I found here, but I thought you'd be more interested in the second one." Ty pointed to the table.

There was a box on the table, but I was unsure what it was. I lifted off the lid and gasped in surprise. Laying inside the box, and wrapped in clean papers as if it had been packed, was the book I had been called to. The one that wanted me to read it.

"But," I said without knowing how to finish my question.

"Mr. Sangre saw me looking at it and told me I could take it to my room. He said he was surprised that they taught slaves to read, but it wasn't uncommon for wealthier families," Ty explained, motioning to me to open the book.

"He thinks you can read it," I repeated. "Can you?"

"No," Ty replied. "Remember how I can barely read your language? My brain isn't wired for reading. Big, tough warrior, no need reading." He puffed out his chest. Like he needed to be bigger to be impressive. Ty was the largest of my time traveling friends, and a lineman on our college football team.

"But if he thought you could read it, then it must be from your time," I deduced. Ty nodded and pointed back to the book.

"We only have a few minutes left, but I wanted you to at least look at it. Can you still read it?" Ty asked.

I glanced over the frail paper. I could read words here and there, but most of it didn't make sense. I had to imagine most of what I saw were names of people or places. I couldn't tell which, and they all looked the same to me. I kept reading further until I found something that I did recognize, my mother's name, Hepa. I looked back at the first section. It had to be the names of a family.

"Do you have a piece of paper?" I asked him. Ty handed me paper and pencil. "I think we just found out where my mother was from. Once we look up who these people are, we will know exactly what time to go to." I scribbled a few of the names down and folded up the paper. We now knew exactly where to go, and hopefully the names would tell us what time period.

I didn't have more time to read, but I wished I did. There had to be more secrets in the text, but it had to wait. We couldn't be late for the dinner. Ty noticed the time and quickly put the book away. He escorted me back to the dinner and didn't leave my side, but my mind was still wandering. My mother's life in the past became more real. It would take more searching, but we could locate her. I had a place to find her. She had to be waiting for me, and I was going to bring her home.

We arrived at the dinner, and I did my best to ignore Logan. He watched me the whole time I ate, but I kept my head turned to Ty to talk only to him. I didn't talk much and just nodded my head when he said something. I wasn't really talkative as I was lost on the names I had copied down. One of them had to be the key. My mother was just steps away from us. It wouldn't take long and we could go get her. One big practice heading back to Ty's time, and then a little more practice and we would be ready to go. I could get my mother back.

Ty arrived early back to my house the day of our planned trip. We would go back into the past, spend some time hiding around his village, and then head home. I didn't know much of what we were getting into, but Ty was sure about it, and I was sure he would take care of everything. He remembered everything about living there, and was sure we could hide around the place as we waited. We didn't know how long it would take before we could travel again, and this was the last little detail we had to get before heading back for my mother.

Ty held my hand with the stone between our palms. We weren't going to take any chances with this travel. I let my mind see the map and globe, and let time spin back at the same time. It was going to have to be Ty to tell me we got it right for sure, but I was getting better at it. As we looked at the Nile we followed it down through Egypt until it began to make curves. We needed to be in the past to be sure where we were going as the Nile had changed over the years, and the areas that Ty knew were flooded in the present. Time was already in the past as we moved along the scenery looking for his village.

Once we got closer to where Ty wanted to be, I zoomed in to look around. Palm trees and agriculture lined the Nile. It was strange to me. I always thoughts of Africa as the desert that housed the Great Pyramids; I didn't picture the lush green land we were hovering over. My views of the past were slowly changing. In the present we only had glimpses of the past, as most of the things from Ty's time were either destroyed or in ruins. Looking at it now, it was all new. Nothing was crumbling and everything was shiny and freshly built. It would take time to get used to seeing everything that way. None of it seem strange to Ty. We traveled further south on the Nile and came across village after village.

"Stop," Ty told me as we passed the fourth village.

I went back and moved even closer. I pictured Ty, and then tried to picture him as a little boy. Time moved again until it found a place to stop that would be closer to where he remembered it.

"Where to?" I asked, looking at the world below us.

His town was nothing like I imagined. He had shown me a few artist renditions of his people in history books in animal print clothing. I guess I assumed they would be living in thatched roof huts in the primitive country side, but that was not the city below. Ty came from a real city. There were mud brick houses reminding me of adobe houses in the southern US. They were spaced some in clumps, but not dense in other parts, and some there wasn't much space between them. The city had to have at least fifty houses of various sizes. A larger building was off to the side between the housing and what must have been a city wall.

"Go nearer to the palace," Ty directed us.

"Palace?" I asked. They all looked the same to me. And why would we need to go to a palace? We planned to just hide out in the village, not greet the king.

Ty shrugged beside me, pulling our linked hands slightly.

"My dad was kind of in charge," Ty finally replied as we looked over what had to be the palace, the largest building around. Ty as a prince was news to me.

The palace was three times the size of the largest house and made with stones along with mud bricks. The courtyard was filled with Egyptian soldiers milling about. Near one corner, darker-skinned men like Ty were kneeling with their hands tied behind them. Why were the men just sitting? I wasn't completely sure what we were looking at as it didn't seem like there was any struggling until I noticed several of the Egyptians there had covered wounds. Ty knew exactly what was going on.

"We tried to stay free of them, but we lost," Ty explained, noticing where I was looking. "We had sent too many people north to help the other cities. By the time the Egyptians got to our village, we were too small in number to defend ourselves. General Paramessu had an easy time with us."

It was hard to look at the men on the ground now, knowing their fate was to go to Egypt as slaves. They ranged from boys younger than us to middle-aged men, well-muscled and doomed to a life of hard labor. I tried to look away, but could not. I saw each face of each man below. I understood war, and spoils of war, but it was nothing I had ever had to see with my own eyes. I was not prepared for it. Ty squeezed my hand.

"Let's go down behind the palace wall, outside it. In the north east bend there on the left." Ty pulled me away from the scene and pointed the position out to me. "There should be enough room for us to stay in the shadows between the palace and the meeting hall."

I looked to exactly where he was directing me and let us float down to our location. I did one last check to be sure we were hidden, and let us appear in the shadows. I looked to be sure Ty was okay after the travel and with me, and had to stifle a laugh. He was dressed in as little as the Egyptians with just a small swatch of fabric around his waist. He didn't look happy to be bare all of a sudden. He smiled at my quiet giggle and pointed to me. I looked down quickly. Thankfully, I was wrapped in a light white fabric that came over my shoulders and covered my chest. I couldn't say the same about all the women we had passed, and was grateful I had my chest covered. It was nice to get a chuckle after the scene I had just saw. This was the funniest part of our travels, and always made both of us laugh. If we went back too far our clothing would change to fit the time period. Ty in a codpiece in Renaissance clothing probably made me laugh the hardest.

When my giggle stopped, Ty took my hand and led the way around the palace wall. We kept to the shadows, hidden from view. Soon we came to a small opening. It wasn't large enough to fit a man, but I bet that Ty was able to come and go as he pleased when he was younger. Ty bent down and looked through the hole. There was a courtyard and several people hustled about. We were still outside the palace, but now could look into another courtyard. Ty watched more, and I bent down behind him to find his focus. A young, beautiful woman sat in the shade with a small infant on her lap. Her hair was all tied up, displaying the elegant line of her neck. She sat as regally as any queen, yet something about her seemed much more real. It was her smile. She called to the children playing around, and they responded with waves and giggles.

"My mother," Ty explained into my ear. The noise in the courtyard alone would cover his voice, but he was still being cautious.

We sat for at least ten minutes watching the young woman with her child. We had not traveled back far enough for Ty to be a baby. I had to assume it was his sibling. Young boys played in the courtyard, and I looked around at each of them. It wasn't hard to see that they were all related, and none of them stood still long enough for me to compare them with Ty.

He smiled at the scene with a heavy heart before nodding to me. We had to go back to our spot before any of the smaller children found us in their escape route. We silently went back to our original location in the shadows.

Voices neared our hiding spot, and Ty pushed me behind him. We flatted against the palace wall as the voices walked past the narrow opening. I didn't see the men from behind Ty, but it was obvious he did see them, and knew them. He took my hand and pulled me further between the tightly built buildings in a different direction than from his mother. Soon we had to crawl as there were openings chest high at the wall beside us. We stopped behind the building next to the palace and sat under one window. We were still hidden, but now heard what was happening inside.

The two men that passed us before were inside the building. They walked to the window we were hidden under. We were near enough to hear the two men speak. I moved quietly to the edge of the window to get a peek and pulled my head back down immediately. There was a large, dark-skinned man that was similar to Ty; I had no doubt who he was. The second man I recognized, too. I would have recognized him anywhere in any time, especially his younger self. Without a doubt the man with Ty's dad was a young general Paramessu. I had only met the general twenty years older, but I knew it was him. He was so similar to Seth, it made my heart ache. It had been over a month now since I saw Seth, and I was missing him terribly. The General made me feel it even worse.

Ty tugged on my hand to get my attention, and we moved down to the next opening on the wall. This one was further up, and we had to stand to peek into the room. We were hidden in darkness as the rest of the room had ample light from strategically placed openings. The two men stood inside talking for only a moment before children were marched into the room.

"And you are sure the pharaoh will take the children in place of the tribute we owe?" Ty's father asked.

"Yes," General Paramessu replied. "I have been instructed to bring back the tribute in food or slaves."

Ty's father nodded and pointed to the line of children. I didn't need Ty to point out which one was him now as they stood still and faced forward. I could tell. The other children played around him, but he watched his father with the strange Egyptian. Ty was young, but his eyes were knowing. The child Ty was as serious as the adult Ty. Ty's father raised his hand and young Ty nodded, ushering all the children over to the two men and closer to our hiding place.

"Which ones will you take?" Ty's father asked as the forty or more children from toddler up to preteen lined up, boys and girl alike.

General Paramessu walked down the line of children. As he pointed to each child, Ty's father nodded and

Egyptians standing at the doorway came and ushered them away. When the General finished on the line, he turned back to Ty's father's side.

"The pharaoh also requests you hand over your son to be sure you will obey, and not try to revolt as the other towns have tried," the general stated. There was no emotion in his voice. It was strange to see a man that looked so much like Seth, but didn't have the spirit of Seth inside him. Seth would have never asked for a child to be taken from his father.

Ty's father reluctantly nodded, like he had been expecting this all along.

"Taraq," Ty's father called to young Ty while dismissing the rest of the children.

Young Ty moved forward and stood in front of his father. He bowed his head and waited to be addressed. He was an obedient child. Ty's father placed an arm around his son and led him a few feet closer to us. The General moved back to his men that were now waiting for the one last child.

"I need you to do something for our people," Ty's father began, keeping his arm around young Ty and bending down to be the young child's height. Young Ty looked up at him with his big brown eyes. He couldn't have been much older than four or five, but I could tell how much he idolized his father. "The general needs to take you back with him. You will understand one day, but I can't explain it all to you now. If you go, our people will survive. If I keep you, we will have to give our supplies of food to them, and they will take every woman and child from our village. I need you to leave and obey the general. In time I hope to bring you home someday. Our debt to the Pharaoh will take many years to pay off, but I'll come myself to bring you back. You will be a man by then, but you will always be my son. Our people will rejoice your return. You will be the prince everyone is waiting for, and will follow in my rule. Please be a dutiful child and learn all you can from the General. He will teach you to be a good man, and thus a good king. Now go off to your mother to say goodbye to her."

"Yes, Father," young Ty replied. He bowed to his father and left. He didn't question what he was told, and was already gone before the two remaining Egyptian army men followed behind the little boy.

Ty moved to crawl away again, probably to follow young Ty in his saying goodbye to his mother, but I didn't join him. The general and Ty's father were talking again. Ty's father moved back over to General Paramessu. They were still within hearing distance for us. Ty waited for me.

"Will that be enough to make the Pharaoh happy?" Ty's father asked. He was concerned about his village, and rightfully so. Seth had told me that there wasn't a battle in the south that General Paramessu didn't win.

"Yes," the General replied and turned to leave Ty's father alone in the large room.

"Just please don't tell my son he can't come home," Ty's father added in a quieter voice. He was king, yet somehow seemed like a defeated man. He had just given away his oldest child and the son he probably dreamed about raising in his own image.

General Paramessu nodded. "I have a son the same age back home. I understand." It was the only hint of emotion I ever saw from him. "I'll take him home, and he will be my son's slave. Don't worry. In time he will forget about you and coming home."

I turned to Ty in the shadows. He was sitting beneath the window on the ground. His face was set in stone. He had truly believed he was coming home when he was a man. That wasn't the case. He was now finding out the truth. He didn't have a home to go back to. They were not waiting for him. He was to be a slave for the rest of his life. I grabbed Ty's hand and held on tight as he closed off his emotions, yet he was still feeling them. His world was crumbling down. I knew the feeling all too well. He squeezed my hand back, strongly, but not enough to hurt me. No matter what was in store for us, I had his back as he had mine. He was my best friend and partner in all of this time travel business.

We sat there for quite a while as Ty forced his emotions off. When the men had finally left the building, it safe enough to speak.

"I'm sorry," I said quietly to him.

I was still afraid of being caught. Not only would I stand out by not fitting in ethnically, but our language would be a dead giveaway that we were not from this time. It was nice the stones allowed us to understand and speak the languages where we traveled, but I still found myself conversing in English. I really was worried that if we got caught right now, with the village invaded by Egyptians, they would add Ty to the roster of grown male slaves they were taking back. Ty needed me to get back to the future. We couldn't be separated now, or who knows where he would end up.

"So am I," Ty replied, standing up. His self-pity party was done. He had just heard devastating news, yet he was back to being my best friend Ty. He was one of the strongest people I knew, both physically and mentally. I don't know how much crying it would have taken me to get over a blow like that.

Ty was back to business and planning our next steps. He led me back between the houses. We had to pause often and let people pass. The village was full, but not many people were out. Most were probably hiding from the Egyptians who marched around freely, and they were our main challenge to avoid. After over an hour of playing go, stop, and hide, we made it to the edge of the village. Ty didn't even pause at his house this time to see his mother and little brother. I had no doubt the truth stung too much, no matter how strong he seemed to be. When we got to the last house on the edge, we sat down in the shadows and waited for nightfall. There was nothing but open grassland and trees beyond the wall. I trusted Ty to know where we were going, and just sat and waited with him. Once it was night and complete darkness, Ty led me into the area outside his home. I was slightly worried about wild animals, but he didn't seem too concerned.

He led me further into the darkness and my eyes adjusted. There was enough moonlight to see by, and we made our way up a hill away from the sounds of the people below. He found a specific grouping of trees and sat down. I sat beside him. When we were finally far enough away to still see the village, but not be seen by them, he talked.

"I never knew," he said quietly, watching over the town he had been longing to go back to for over a decade.

I looked up at his lost eyes. His world had changed with this one trip. The goddess' warning had played in my mind again. Every trip has a price. Traveling through time changes things. Even without directly interacting with his past, it still changed things. Ty was changed. His world wasn't the world he thought it was. He was never coming back to this place a free man. He could never go home. In one little trip, he lost his family and his hope.

"We need to get back to my time," I told him. I looked down at my arm. In the moonlight I could make out that the lines were not filled enough to travel. Ty nodded, but saw the truth. We were going to have to stay a while longer.

"Get some sleep," Ty told me, wrapping an arm around me and pulling me close to lean against him. "I'll keep watch."

For once I didn't ask, but I did as he told me. I was exhausted from the travel more than I ever expected to be, but it was going to be hard to sleep as my mind was still thinking of what to do. Everything we had planned thus far wasn't going to work. I couldn't bring Ty back to the past to live if he was just going to stay a slave. I wasn't sure how he felt, but I just couldn't do it. Now we had to go back and replan everything. Our original thought of saving my mother, and then going back to be with Seth and Dee wasn't in the cards now. I had to protect Ty. Even though we could travel into the past, we needed a new plan. I closed my eyes and tried to think of options. Nothing came to me but the haze of sleep.

Birds were chirping when I finally opened my eyes to find it was morning. I had no clue when I drifted off in my thoughts, but the sun had risen, and Ty was still sitting there watching the town. I couldn't tell if he had slept or not.

We were seated in an area a little up from the village to the northwest. It gave us a clear view of the entire town and the activity below us. I watched as the Egyptian men, with their lighter skin and swath of white fabric around their waists, ushered darker-skinned men away from the town. I could barely make out the men walking as they were lost from our view. Ty was watching. We sat in silence as the last of the Egyptians left the village. Right here was when Ty's life changed forever, both in the past and watching it now.

"I want to stay in the future," Ty told me as he helped me stand.

I looked down at my arm. The lines were full. We could go home. And it was home now for Ty. His heart, that had longed to be in the village below, had changed. I took his hand and held on tight. We were heading home.

CHAPTER 6

CHANGING PLANS

I looked across my desk to Ty. Papers were scattered around everywhere. His small, distinct writing was on some of the pages and my more girly handwriting was on most. Small papers and large papers were intertwined. It was one large mess. We had spent hours making the notes and knew exactly where my mother was, what time period, and what country, we even knew which city she would be located in. There were notes on everything from food to clothing to political systems, yet we couldn't agree what to do.

"I can't take you with me," I told Ty for the twentieth time. "If we get separated, you won't be able to come back. I can't do that to you. You already told me you want to stay here, and we know what your fate will be if you stay there."

"I do want to stay here, but I have to help. I know that time better than you. You'll need me," Ty replied. "And I promised Seti," he added quietly.

I sighed and shook my head. He wanted to be free of his past, yet he was still just as loyal to Seth as he was when he lived there. He wasn't free, and wouldn't let himself be.

Ty made a great protective older brother, but at this point I wanted to smack him over the head and run off. It was time he let me protect him.

"If I take Dee's stone and go back, you don't have to worry. I won't have to wait to recharge my carnelian if I get in trouble. I can just use Dee's chrysoprase. And if everything goes according to plan, then I use the chrysoprase to bring my mother back," I explained for what seemed like the umpteenth time. My plan had logic and a back-up plan. I would be safe.

"I don't like you going off alone to a time you don't understand yet," Ty argued with my solution. He wasn't debating how it would work. There was too much logic behind my plan. Instead, he used the *I don't like it* response. "And you're female. You don't understand what it's like to be female back then."

I pointed to all the papers on the desk. "What is there left to know? I'm not going to go there to live. I'm just going there to get my mother and bring her home. I don't need to know anything beyond how to grab her and time travel back."

"You could get trapped there. You could end up no where near your mother, and have to get to her in a city you don't understand. You could end up hurt, kidnapped, or even taken by traders to sell," Ty replied. "I still don't like it."

"And neither do I," Logan said as he shimmered into the room.

"You were right," he said to Ty. "Your mother was returned to her people by the Egyptians, yet her cousin, who is in charge, still thinks it's a ploy. If you go in and take your mother away, they will think the Egyptians took her again. They will attack the Egyptian men in the city, and your precious Seth happens to be right there."

My mouth must have been hanging open as he chuckled at me. I really didn't want to see Logan again.

He was too confusing, and didn't seem to take the hint that I wasn't interested in him anymore. Logan was convinced that Seth had moved on, and that I should be with him, but even if that was true I still couldn't turn to Logan. I didn't trust him, and I didn't feel the same for him as I felt for Seth.

"Ty asked me to head back and see what the situation was," Logan explained his presence.

I turned my back to Logan and gave Ty a look to say *what the heck are you doing bringing Logan into this?* He got my message and shrugged.

"Have you told her your plan?" Logan asked Ty.

"Yes, Ty, have you told me your plan?" I mocked Logan with a bit of anger.

Ty smiled meekly at me. He had told Logan more than I was willing to at this point, and he knew how I felt about Logan. Guys were annoying. I hated that guys could move on so fast from arguments. It was only weeks ago that Ty punched Logan and likely broke his nose. Now they seemed to be buddies again. Dumb boys.

"Logan and I thought that it might be best to go in and bring everyone back at once," Ty replied, begging my forgiveness with his eyes. I turned from him and glared at Logan. I still wasn't happy with him, and I really didn't want him in on the planning with us. I didn't need to owe Logan any favors.

"You know I can only travel with one person, and we only have one extra stone," I replied, shooting down their plan immediately. That meant we could only take home two people, not the three we left behind.

"With Logan's help we can get more than one because Logan can travel back twice to get two people," Ty replied. My eyes had to bug open at that. We were just fighting not even two minutes ago about how he wouldn't let me go alone. If Logan was going back and forth, I would be left alone at some point.

"I can take one person at a time and come back immediately for the other person," Logan replied, like he was making completely logical sense.

I looked between them. They were both nodding together. They had already agreed on what to do, and were just waiting for me to jump on board with their plans. Was Ty really suggesting I go off alone with Logan again? It didn't end too well the last time. I really didn't want a second round.

"Can we talk alone?" I asked Ty. Logan smiled and nodded before fading away.

Ty waited on my bed for me to say something. I marched over to him and realized that I stood only a little taller than him when he was sitting. I just stared at him, looking for the reason he was suggesting such an idea.

"Did you forget my last travels with Logan?" I asked Ty finally.

"I talked to him about it. He said it was a *one time lapse in judgment*," Ty replied, trying to mimic Logan's voice, which was higher than his own bass voice. "It won't happen again. He promised that he is trying to help you get to Seti. This is his way to make it up to you."

"And I'm to just trust him?" I asked. *And trust myself alone with him*, I wanted to add.

"Mari. I can't have you going off alone on this. Logan can help, and get everyone home. If he is with you then you won't be alone, and all the danger I'm imagining can't happen. Anything bad happens, and he'll whisk you away back here. Your protection had always been his priority," Ty replied. "Why don't we just let him help?"

"Because I still don't know *why* he's helping. What does he get out of it?" I tapped my fingers on my desk as I sat there.

"He just wants to help. And we need help. You don't want to let me go, and I don't want to let you go alone. We need to do something," Ty replied. "This is a compromise because we can't agree."

It was true that we couldn't agree. He was right. We were at a standstill, but I wasn't sure that Logan was the solution. There had to be another way. I had hesitations about Logan helping. I already knew that there was another Logan, who wasn't the one I knew two years ago. This new Logan would take people and leave them in other times. Now that I knew how Logan felt about me, I doubted he would take me to Seth or help Seth come back here. That didn't seem like the new Logan's style.

"Just let him explain his plan," Ty replied. "If you don't like it, then we start over and figure our own way on it. It can't hurt to listen." Ty was being too persuasive. He had to already know Logan's plan.

"Fine, but I refuse to do anything alone with Logan. If Logan comes with me, he follows behind me where I don't see him, or have to interact with him," I replied. It was a bad idea to involve Logan, but maybe that was just me trying to avoid the confusing feelings between us.

"I can do that," Logan said as he reappeared. I was beginning to hate how he could come and go as he pleased.

"What is your plan?" I asked.

I had to humor Ty even though I wasn't sure I wanted to work with Logan on anything. Logan grinned at my question. *Nope, I really didn't want to work with him.* It was a bad idea to trust him.

"You travel to your mother. Once you find her, call for me. I'll be around, but not alone with you as per your request. I can go instantly to Seth and Dee. I'll have Ty's stone with me so that I can bring them both. It will only take me a moment to bring them back here with me and then I'll return to help you take your mother back. You will only be left alone one moment with your mother, who knows the time period exactly," Logan explained.

Ty looked at me hopefully. Logan's plan met all of Ty

requirements, and if he was willing to just follow me, and not touch me, then it met mine, too. I didn't have an argument against it.

"I go in and find my mom, and then we just leave?" I asked. That sounded a bit too simple. When I traveled I needed time to recover. Logan had to know that much.

"I'll take you to the past to your mother, and then I'll take each person back, including you if needed," Logan replied, seeing my dilemma.

"And when would we do all this?" I asked.

"Today works for me," Logan replied. Ty nodded. Easy for him, he would just sit here and wait for us to come back.

"Meet us back here in one hour," Ty suggested, seeing that I wasn't completely ready. It wouldn't take an hour for me to be ready, but the less time with Logan, the better. Logan nodded and was gone again.

"Why one hour?" I asked Ty after Logan left.

"Because we need to plan a little more," Ty replied, the conclusion was obvious to him, not me.

"Plan? I thought you approved of the Logan plan." I eyed him over. What game was he playing? Either Ty was with Logan or not. Couldn't he make up his mind?

"Oh, I trust Logan to keep you safe. Like I said, he looks at you just like Seti does. I just don't trust him to care if he gets Dee or Seti back here, too," Ty replied. I breathed a sigh of relief. Ty wasn't completely fooled by the angel Logan was pretending to be.

"Then what is your back-up plan?" I asked, knowing by the look on Ty's face that he already had one.

Ty stood and went to my nightstand drawer.

"This," he said, pulling out the green chrysoprase stone. I did wonder why Logan said he'd take Ty's stone and not the extra stone. I hadn't told Logan about Dee's stone, but I figured that Ty had mentioned it to him in all their planning. I must have been wrong. "I'm not about to let him have it. You should have seen how his eyes lit up when I told him he could use the stone I used to get here, since I never wanted to go back. He didn't snatch it out of my hand, but he looked like he was going to. I don't think the gatekeepers are supposed to use the stones, but because he can, I think Logan likes having them in his possession."

"Then I'll take the extra stone. It still doesn't help me get everyone back here," I replied, looking at the stone in Ty's hand.

"But it gives you an out if you need it. And more so, once you find your mother, you can send her home. We will figure out how to get Seti and Dee once you're back, if everything falls apart. I just figured by including Logan we stood a chance to get everyone here at once. Without him, it was bound to end badly. I don't exactly want to work with him, either. I don't trust him. But I know he will protect you," Ty said, explaining his reasoning and making me feel a bit better about everything.

I stood up and moved over to the bed next to Ty to hug him.

"I'd take you with me if I knew you would be safe, but we know it's dangerous for you there. You need to stay here. You need to stay free," I said as I hugged him. He patted my back.

"You know I'm meant to be the one to protect you," Ty replied. "Not the other way around."

"Ty, you're my best friend. I'll do anything to keep you safe, just like my mother, Seth, and Dee. You are all family in this weird time travel world. I'll get everyone back, and I will be safe." I sat back and looked at him to make sure he understood. Ty shook his head with a laugh.

"I know you will." Ty handed me the apple green stone in his hand. "I'd feel a lot better if this stone was permanently on your arm like the other one."

A wind blew through the air and the papers on my desk

scattered. I looked around for an open door or window, but knew there would be none. It was winter in Chicago. Yes, it was the windy city, but I was pretty sure you had to be outside to feel it. This was a different type of breeze, and one I was getting used to by now.

"And so would I," a ghostly female voice came into the room.

Ty immediately bowed his head to the dusty form appearing in front of us. I stared up at her. It may be rude to stare, but I couldn't help it. I had talked to the goddess after Thanksgiving, but there was something about seeing her again. Her form was just as awe-inspiring as the first time I saw her, but her ghostly figure just was not as bright as I remembered. Her body was made of floating sparkles that caught the light in the room just right. She looked like a glittery human ghost, yet somehow more beautiful and not as scary.

"You would what?" I asked. I wasn't going to bow to her like Ty. She took away my family, and I wanted them back.

She smiled at me and held out her hand. "The chrysoprase."

I handed the stone over to her. She took it and took hold of the arm that already had the carnelian on it. Soon dust poured from her hand. She swirled a new pattern on my arm with the green powder. It burned momentarily, and then it was embedded into my arm like the first stone.

"But..." I tried to argue. With her perfect timing, she had to know what I was up to. She told me I had to accept the past, and here I was going against it.

"I believe you will do what is right. You will see I'm not the bad guy," the goddess said in her musical voice. Ty peeked up at her, but instantly lowered his head again. "Even you, Taraq, have a role to play in this time and the past. Don't give up on your father. Sometimes parents must make the most heart-wrenching decisions."

"Yes, goddess," Ty replied, his voice a bit stiff. Her words had made him think more.

"I still don't understand," I replied, looking at the new light green lines. They were intertwined with the brownish red lines, but formed their own pattern.

"You will, in time," the goddess replied before vanishing as quickly as she came.

Ty looked up at me, and I looked at him. I had no idea what it all meant, but I didn't have time to wonder. Logan was fading back into the room. It wasn't safe to talk around him. Our planning time was over. It was time to go back to get my mother.

Logan stood near me. I refused to take his arm. He placed a hand on my shoulder like he did when he traveled with Ty. This time I didn't need to know exactly where I was traveling, since Logan was going to direct us to the spot, and I needed to save my stone for my escape from the past. I was going along with him, but I refused to hold onto him. He promised to drop me off with my mother before going to get Seth and Dee.

We began our travels, and I got to see how he went through what he taught me. Our connection brought me into his time travel world. We floated above the earth as the globe spun to the Middle East. Zooming in and going back in time simultaneously, which I had yet to master, we came upon a large city. Brown and white mud brick homes spanned miles, each not much bigger than my bedroom, and all connected. They opened to curved streets that wove around the city in odd shapes. Far in the distance, yet surrounded by all the squat buildings, was a large, walled-off palace. The stone walls stood stories above the city, whether from being on a hill or just being larger, it was difficult to tell. Logan moved us toward the palace, and my nerves set in. I hadn't seen my mom in a long time, and I was worried what she would think of me coming back to get her. I was even more worried to find her okay and happy in the past. Then I'd have to leave and go home without her.

I watched our approach to the palace and felt sick from all the mixed feelings. I wanted to see my mother badly, but now I wasn't sure we planned enough. Would I get her home? Would she even want to go home? Could I do this?

My hand began to tingle in the familiar rush that took over my body. I knew exactly what it meant. Logan wasn't lying about bringing us back, because Seth was in the city and close by. Seth was actually here. The person I had been waiting months to see was somewhere down below in the masses of people. I couldn't help but pull away from Logan. I recognized exactly where I where I wanted to go. I knew precisely what would make me feel better. I needed Seth.

Without Logan behind me, I looked at the buildings beneath me. I hovered over each, seeing how the carnelian lines reacted. There was one in particular that drew me, and I knew Seth was inside. I found a dark side street next to the building without anyone around and let myself appear. I was in the past, and Seth was only feet away.

It wasn't the smartest thing to do, but I couldn't help myself. When I felt the tingles, and knew Seth was near, I needed to be with him. I had been missing him for months after my short visit into the past, and just knowing he was there made me change my course. Our plans to rescue my mother would have to change again, but I was fine with that if I was able to be with him. I still didn't know how much I could trust Logan, but I trusted Seth completely, and wanted to see him, even if I still needed to go get my mom. I was sure he and I could figure that out together.

I felt the heat instantly as I appeared in the shadows. It had to be summertime now, and I wasn't ready for it coming from winter. He was inside the building I was hiding by. The small alleyway wasn't much, but it was at least shaded from the sun and passing people, and there were lots of passing people. The noise alone was surprising, not to mention the colors. I wasn't expecting so much color since I thought I'd be in a desert again. It was a visual feast for my eyes, not to mention a cacophony to my ears. The building I was standing by had to be some sort of eatery judging by the smells that wafted out of it. I peered around the corner of the building. The cloth hanging as a door was pushed back, and I ducked back into the shadows. I couldn't see who exited, but I couldn't show my face the way I was. I had no idea where my mother was at this point. The fact that I looked like her could be either bad or good. I screwed up everything by letting go of Logan. I had once again changed our plans. I had to learn to concentrate better with this time travel ability. At least Seth was nearby. I could feel the tingles shoot down my arm. My stomach flip-flopped knowing that he was just around the corner.

CHAPTER 7

FINDING HOME

"**What are you** doing here?" a rich voice that brought back many memories asked me. I looked up into Seth's chocolate brown eyes. He was concerned, but just as happy to see me as I was him.

"I love you," I blurted out immediately. I needed him to know that. I didn't tell him before when I was in the past with him, and who knew when I'd disappear from him again.

His hands wrapped around me and ushered me to the wall as he didn't respond, but greeted me with his lips upon mine. He pressed me against the building and deepened the kiss. His hands held me tight, pressing the abundant cloth I was wearing to my sweating body. As a few more people left the eatery and passed by us. I hear some sort of words exchanged with Seth, yet his lips never left mine. He gestured to them, and they laughed, and kept walking. When he finally pulled back, he stayed only inches from my face, staring into my eyes.

"It's been too long," he said huskily, staring at my lips again. He tasted of something sweet and fermented, but I was sure he wasn't drunk.

"How long has it been for you?" I asked. The passage of time wasn't the same for the both of us. I looked to his lips and wanted them back also.

"Six months," he replied. I was distracted by his perfect mouth as he talked. He had gone without me longer, but I missed him just as much. "I didn't know if I'd ever see you again." He sounded hurt. It had been too long.

I leaned forward and pulled his head down to meet mine. I kissed him again. I needed to. I needed to feel that he was real. Each time he went away, and my memories changed, it felt like I lost a part of him. In losing him, I was losing part of me. He was everything I ever wanted. It was scary to feel that way about one person, but it was true. Even Logan and our past couldn't compare with the feelings floating around inside me at just the touch of Seth's lips to mine. He was everything I needed.

"And you?" he asked as he pulled back a little.

"Me what?" I asked, looking up into his eyes. The desire I saw there was surely mirrored in my own.

"How long has it been in your time?" Seth asked as he eyed me over, looking for any change in me.

"Five weeks," I replied, watching his eyes roam over my body. When most men looked at you like that it was creepy, but the way he looked made my stomach tumble.

"And Ty was with you there?" Seth asked, finally bringing his eyes up to mine.

"Yes," I answered, looking up at him. Did he really want to just talk after all this time apart?

"But he didn't come with you," Seth replied to my answer.

He balanced on the wall with only one hand, allowing his free hand to reach up and touch my face. I closed my eyes and tried to memorize his touch. No matter how I was with him now, it would never last. I had a feeling we would always have to fight to be together.

"No," I responded, feeling his body press up against

me. His lips met mine again, and I rested my hands on his bare chest. There were a few perks to the Egyptian military clothing, or rather lack of clothing.

"Why," Seth began as he moved his kisses to my ear. "Are." He kissed down my neck, sending tingles to my toes. "You." He reached the indent where my neck and shoulder met. "Here?"

He finished asking his question, but the kisses continued as he pushed the fabric of the multiple tunics I wore out of the way to continue kissing down a line. He began moving back up my neck slowly as he waited for a response, but I was having trouble even remembering the question. It was hard to carry on a conversation when we couldn't keep ourselves apart.

My mind was on a sensory overload just being able to finally touch Seth, and I couldn't think of an answer to his question. Right at that moment, all I could think of was being with him. He was why I was here, but I was sure I was there for something else, too, maybe. I pressed my lips against his bare chest, and he wrapped his free arm around my back to hold me to him. I'd remember eventually what I needed to do in the past, maybe when I remembered to breathe correctly, but at that moment I didn't want his kisses to stop.

"How did you get back here?" Seth asked, all in one breath, before kissing me again.

This conversation thing was really getting hard to do. I smiled as he trailed kisses down my neck again, allowing me to talk, but thinking was hard to do. His question went right out my ears, and I giggled at the butterflies in my stomach he was giving me.

"A stone?" he suggested an answer.

"Kind of," I replied, pulling his lips back up to mine.

"Kind of?" Seth asked, his mouth still stuck to mine.

"Umm," someone said from behind us as the person coughed again. I vaguely remembered hearing him cough the first time. "Seti?"

Seth pulled back to turn his head to the intruding person and caught his breath. I wasn't the only one who needed to remember to breathe correctly. I smiled at him. I was happy that his reaction to seeing me this time was much better than the last time. Then he was mad, now at least he was happy. I hoped it wasn't just the booze in him.

"Yes, Dee?" Seth said, without turning any further than to keep his eyes on me. He kept his eyes glued to me like I might just up and disappear.

"Dee?" I said, standing up straighter and looking beyond Seth's shoulder.

Dee gave a sigh of relief upon seeing me. I smiled at him and gave him a little wave from the hand that was already around Seth's back. I was actually happy to see him too. Seth's best friend had done everything to save me from the men that wanted to use me to force Egypt into war. I thought Dee had betrayed Seth when he helped those men kidnap me, but he was actually a better friend than I could have ever imagined. He even gave me his chrysoprase stone to get to the future again, the green one that now joined the carnelian lines on my arm.

"Glad to see you under him," Dee said, and then shook his head at his own words. His cheeks turned bright red when he realized what he said. "I mean, glad to see you there as I was worried he was drunk and passed out standing up again."

I looked up to Seth. He shrugged. I guess he wasn't having as much fun in his time apart as I imagined him having.

"He's been moping since we reached the city months ago. He spent all his time thinking about you, and trying to find a way back to you when he wasn't drunk," Dee explained when Seth did not.

Seth looked over his shoulder at Dee. It must have been a man exchange as Dee reddened again.

"I was coming to find you to make sure you came back early tonight. Prince Saru has summoned us to the palace tomorrow to tell us his decision. If you showed up hung over again, he would be mad. We stand a better chance if you're sober before the prince, if we stand any chance at all," Dee explained quickly, he finally realized he was still interrupting us.

Seth nodded and waved his hand to dismiss Dee. "So be it."

Dee left to stand at the end of the darkened walkway we were in, and we were back to essentially being alone. Seth turned to me and smiled. He saw me staring at Dee, and I turned back to him. Instead of resuming our greeting, he confused me by backing up a little.

"No more welcome home kisses?" I pouted. I didn't quite have my fill of him yet, if it was even possible for me to ever get my fill.

Seth pulled me from the wall and grinned. After studying my clothing for a moment, he took the loose fabric hanging over my shoulder and pulled it over my head. He nodded to himself and then took my hand.

"How about we catch up somewhere more private, without an audience," Seth hinted at Dee. I thought Dee was going to go eventually, but I guess he wasn't going to leave us alone, ever the dutiful soldier.

I looked at Dee with his back to us, and the passing people that kept walking by. I had just been making out with Seth in broad daylight with tons of people passing by. At any moment people could see us there. It was dark in the walkway, but not that dark. I wasn't one for public displays of affection, but that seemed to go out the door once Seth looked at me. I wasn't too concerned about the people walking by anymore, but it would be nice to really be alone with him and we needed to talk. There was much I had to tell him that didn't need to be heard by a passerby.

I finally let him pull me away from my hiding place as my answer.

"Won't they question an Egyptian soldier walking off with a local girl?" I asked, pointing to my clothing and then his. We certainly didn't belong together. He was in his small, white military skirt, and I wore several tunics similar to the women who passed by on the street. We did make a strange couple compared to the others who only grouped together with similarly-dressed people.

Seth smiled. "If they knew who you were they might worry, but around here no one is going to give you a second glance, as long as you keep your head down. Soldiers hook up with women in the various cities we visit all the time."

Hooked up? Great. They were all going to think I was a prostitute. I never imagined pretending to be that role before.

"Keep your hair covered, and as much of your skin as you can. Anyone as pale as you with that hair would be assumed to be royalty, and I don't need you making a scene for us. Who knows what anyone would do if they thought or knew as much," Seth explained. "Keep your face down, and I'll lead. Dee will follow behind us." Seth waited for my response before he would move.

I nodded, and he began to walk. I looked down at the dirt, even though my instinct was to look around me. I couldn't even tell where we were heading, or how to get anywhere, not that it would matter being that I had no clue where I was to begin with. It was hard to keep my head down as I wondered about where I was. I was curious by nature and this new adventure made me want to know more. But I needed to stay safe. The only anchor I had was Seth's hand, and I trusted him completely.

The world I had just traveled into was far different than what I was expecting. The Egyptians I had met were in their sterile white linen and polished armor. This world was much more colorful as women and men both passed in colors other than white. I could only stare at the hems of their tunics and their shoes as we passed. Seth kept us moving forward through bends the twists of the street. Normally I'd be concerned by not knowing where I was going, but holding Seth's hand was reassurance enough that I was safe.

Soon we stopped at another building. I glanced up at it before looking back down again. This one was two stories tall, and noisy even from the outside. Seth pushed back the cloth doorway and walked into the large open room. I glanced up to see the inside, but Dee bumped me to remind me to look back down. Seth led us through the tables and chairs scattered around the room. They were mostly filled with rowdy men. A few women walked in between. Seth didn't stop to talk to any of the people, but many made jeers at me and him as we passed. Seth didn't acknowledge anyone.

We made it through the rowdy room and passed through another doorway. This led to stairs and the second floor. The second floor was much quieter than the ground level, and I barely heard the singing and talking down below. That was until Seth opened one of the doors that lined the hallway, and the noise traveled through the open window into the room. Seth pulled me in behind him. Dee halted outside the door.

Seth nodded to Dee and moved to shut the door, but I stopped him before he could.

"Thanks, Dee," I said.

I never did have a chance to thank him the last time I was in the past when he gave me his stone to get me to the future. Dee smiled and nodded before walking away. He could see in Seth's eyes what I already saw. Seth wanted to be alone with me. It normally would have scared me to be alone with a guy, but it didn't scare me with Seth.

Seth shut the door and tugged on my bulky tunic. I

turned to find myself already in his arms. He pulled me down to the bed and onto his lap.

"You came without Ty," Seth said, almost like he was scolding me.

"Um, yeah, about that," I said while keeping my arms around him. "There was a plan about saving my mother and you guys. I kind of messed it up."

Seth raised his eyebrows. "Do tell," he replied.

"I kind of got distracted when I knew you were here," I answered, looking into his chest to keep myself from seeing his reaction. It wasn't like me to not follow through on a plan. I was a little embarrassed that I had let emotion take over.

There was a fresh scar beneath my hand. I looked back up to Seth, forgetting that I was embarrassed.

"What happened?" I asked of the red line that ran just under his ribs.

"I spent a little too much time with your captors," Seth replied. "They found us after you left. There wasn't anywhere else to hide in those caves, and they just sent more people into them. They were desperate to have you. When I couldn't tell them where you were, they didn't think I was worth keeping around, eating their supplies." Seth shrugged like being carved up wasn't a big deal, and to him it probably wasn't now that we were back in the past. I bent down and kissed the raised scar.

"I'm sorry," I said as tears began to well up. I had caused this to happen to him. If I had planned more, and knew what I was doing, I could have found a better way to Seth. I could have stopped my mother from leaving me. It was all my doing. I had messed up then, and technically I messed up again now by letting go of Logan and changing the plan.

Seth pulled my face up to his. "This isn't your fault," he scolded me. "The fact that you would come back into the past for me has kept me going. You keep me going. I'd have given up a long time ago if it weren't for you. My life was planned out for me. My dad was going to marry me off. I was to have children and keep the family line going. It was never about love. You are the reason I have ever known what true love is. Never be sorry for being you." He held my face between his hands and stared deep into my eyes. His chocolate brown eyes were filled with love. He meant every word he said.

Tears spilled down my cheeks, and he rubbed them away. "I thought you would move on without me," I whispered my deepest fear to him. I truly had believed Logan's word.

"Never," Seth replied. "I can't breathe without you. I could never move on. You are the light in my world. No matter where you go, or if you never come back, you are all I ever want. There is nowhere I can move on to."

I hiccupped a little as my tears flowed. They were for both relief and happiness now. I had my doubts when I was in the future. I had only known Seth for a few months, and had spent most of them avoiding him and his plays to win me over. I never was sure if it was really love he felt for me, or just the thrill of conquest since I was the only girl that ever turned him down. Seth held my face and wiped more tears away. They were slowing down. He stared intensely at me.

"Marcella Navina, I swear before the gods that you are the only girl for me. I love you with every bit of my body and soul, and will never love another in life or death. I was serious when I told my father we should get married. I will never marry another. You are already bound to my heart tighter than any marriage could ever be," Seth declared. A breeze swirled into the room and then out again as if the goddess had heard his declaration and approved. My heart beat fast. There were no doubts now.

I leaned in and kissed him, pulling our bodies as close as I could while I was on his lap. I couldn't form words as pretty as his to tell him that he meant the same to me. He had summed up exactly what I was feeling inside. I needed to show him. I untied the belt around the overtunic I wore. Seth lifted it over my head, stopping the kiss only long enough to get it off me. I was left in the lighter, white under tunic as he laid me on the bed. Seth hovered above me, balancing on his arms on either side of my head as his lips never left mine.

Having no clue how any of the odd clothing either of us were wearing worked, I tugged at the waistband of the kilt-like, linen wrap-around skirt he wore.

Seth pulled back just inches from my face and looked deep into my eyes.

"Are you sure?" he asked, ever the gentleman.

I pulled his face back to mine with one hand, and reached down and tugged again at the only thing covering him with my other hand. I didn't know how much time I had in the past. I didn't know what the next moment would bring. I didn't know if I could even save my mother. But I did know that I wanted to be with Seth. I needed to be with Seth. He declared his love for me before the gods and in my heart I felt the exact same way. Our world together would always be a mystery, but I didn't have to be alone in that mystery. Seth would always be there for me. We were meant to be together.

I woke sometime during the night when the noise below finally was gone. It was too silent. I had no idea what time it was beyond early morning, but I did know where I was. I was still in Seth's arms. We had been alone all day making memories that would last a lifetime if needed. Only a thin sheet covered our naked bodies. The night air had cooled from the day's harsh sun. I was tucked into Seth's arm, and his body provided the rest of the heat to keep me warm. Seth kissed my forehead.

"You're awake?" I asked quietly.

"I wasn't," he replied a little gruffly, like he just woken up, too. "Are you warm enough?" he asked, tucking me closer to him.

I was definitely warm enough, but I wasn't going to pull away from him, or tell him otherwise. I didn't want his body to move. His bare skin rubbed against mine, making me blush a little from the thoughts of our day and night together, and it made my stomach do flips. With one little touch he could make a host of emotions run through me. Seth chuckled as he could see my face with the faint sunrise lighting up our room slightly.

Seth kissed the tip of my nose.

"How did you know I was there yesterday outside the bar?" I asked. I had been wondering about it. The carnelian lines on my arm directed me to him, but how did he know to come outside at that exact moment.

He grinned. "Fate," he answered. I pushed back from him a little. "Okay, okay. When you're around, I feel it. I can tell if you're angry, scared, happy, excited." Seth's finger trailed down my arm, causing goose bumps to form and my heart to beat faster. "The goddess told me I would know when I found you. I asked her to explain, and she said that I would just know. I do just know. It's like how I imagine music would feel, not hearing with your ears, but feeling with your hands. I feel like that when you are around. We're fated to be together. The goddess was right."

I smiled. He was just as attached to me as I was to him.

"And you feel something, too, don't you," Seth deduced.

"Yeah," I admitted. He was right, we were meant to be together. "The carnelian lines tingle when I'm close to you, like they want us to be together."

Seth pulled me in tight before releasing me to talk more.

"We're meant to be together. I will fight to be with you until my last breath," Seth swore to me.

I stared into his eyes and saw he was very serious. The guy I thought was just another player turned out to be someone else. Seth was far more than just another guy. He was *the* guy for me. I'd fight to be with him. The goddess brought us together for a reason, and I was unsure if I ever would find out why, but I knew one thing for certain: I was glad she did. We belonged together.

"And I'll fight to be with you," I replied. I touched his face gently and he smiled. He took my hand and kissed each of my fingertips.

"Now, are you going to explain these lines to me?" he asked, my hand still in his.

I laughed. I had meant to explain the lines to him earlier, but we just didn't spend too much time on them. I think I remembered the conversation as, *these are new, uh-huh,* and that was it. Even after spending all day together, there hadn't been many words spoken.

"Your stone," I told him, using his finger to trace the deep red line in my arm. "Dee's stone." I traced the green lines next.

"Those are the chalcedony stones?" Seth asked, holding my arm gently and looking closer at the lines.

"Yes. The goddess said that since I can travel, she doesn't want me to get stuck. She put the carnelian stone in my arm before I came the last time, and the chrysoprase stone this time," I answered.

Seth held my arm up so that the sunlight could catch on it. There was a faint sparkle to the lines.

"You're a goddess now," Seth said reverently.

"What?" I asked, looking at him and then the line. "No, no, no. Not even close," I added.

Seth shook his head. "You carry the magic of the

goddess within you now. You are a goddess."

I wasn't sure how to argue with that. The lines were there, plain as day, and they did contain the magic of the goddess. But to me, that didn't make me a goddess. It made me the person wearing the magic, just like the necklace Seth wore when I first met him.

Seth leaned back close to me and kissed my forehead again when I couldn't come up with an argument against him. He smiled like he'd won, and slipped out of bed.

He stood up and wrapped his shendyt, as he called it, back around his naked body. I stayed in bed and just watched him. I was distracted from arguing as I gazed at him. He was perfection from head to toe. Every part of his body was formed as if he had been molded out of clay by a sculptor. I watched the toned muscles in his arms move to wrap skirt around him. It sat low, just on the hips, and I could still see the indents where the muscles connected at the hip bones.

Seth caught me staring and grinned at me. He crossed the room in two strides and bent down to kiss me.

"I'll be right back," he said, tugging at the covers I now used to cover my body. "And don't you dare move from this spot. For anything," he ordered, and I got his point. He had seen me eye up my clothing. It wasn't like I was sure how to put the under tunic back on anyways.

Seth left the room and I settled back into the bed. It wasn't the most comfortable bed I ever slept in, but I would have been happy to never leave it, if Seth was going to keep me company. Days in bed sounded good to me now. I had screwed up all our plans anyways, and it wasn't like it mattered if I took my time with Seth. I was sure Logan was looking for me, but I didn't care. I'd stay with Seth as long as I could.

Seth came back into the room carrying a tray with bowls of steaming food on it.

"Breakfast in bed for the love of my life," Seth declared

as I sat up.

It hit me as I watched him. I was in some run-down little inn in the middle of a city I didn't remember the name of, in a time I shouldn't have even existed in. Everything about it was too surreal, yet Seth sat down beside me and opened up dishes of food I couldn't recognize, like it was normal for us to be sitting around like this. It was peaceful and just seemed right, as this was the life we were meant to have together. Seth didn't notice, but I did. This was meant to be our life. We were meant to go on adventures together, and we were meant to be happy, just as we were now.

"You'd like that one," Seth said, pointing to what I'd describe as off-white, speckled mush. "And the dates." Seth pointed to the brownish, nut-looking things beside the mush.

I tried each. I knew what dates were, but had never tried them before. They had a very sweet, almost nutty, flavor with the texture of raisins. I was really surprised, because they didn't look like they would taste good. The white mush turned out to be some sort of grain cooked up with spices. While it wasn't sweet, obviously they didn't use sugar like present-day meals tended to, it was good anyway.

"What was the plan you messed up?" Seth finally asked. We had to finally talk. I hated to go back to reality.

I wanted details from him, but it looked like I'd have to tell my tales first. As we ate, I told him everything about the past five weeks; my mother missing, learning how to time travel, and even Logan. There would be no secrets between us. Seth listened intently, laughed, smiled, and even showed a bit of anger when I told him about Logan. By telling him everything, it made it feel like he was a part of it all. I saw how he wanted to be able to experience it with me, but we were together now and that was all that mattered.

"And what about you?" I finally asked after my story was done.

"My time wasn't as much fun as yours," Seth said, setting the food aside. "When Dee finally got my father's rescue team to me, I was in pretty bad shape. I don't remember a few weeks there."

My heart broke. Seth was in the past where there was no modern medicine or cures, and he had been sick from saving me. I couldn't bear to think of him like that. It wasn't fair. Seth caught the sadness in my eyes and pulled me to him. What if he hadn't made it? What if I returned to the past sometime, and found him no longer in it?

"Mari. I told you. I'll survive anything because I want to be with you," Seth added quietly, stroking my head as I rested it on his chest.

"When I got better, I found out that your mother had suddenly appeared like you had. My father ordered me to bring her back here. I don't know what was said between my father and your mother, but my father knew her," Seth said, leaning me back on the bed. "My job was to bring her back and ask to have her marry the current Pharaoh like she had been promised to the previous one."

"You want to take her back to Egypt?" I asked. I had never pictured my mother anywhere in the past but where we were now. I guess I thought she was past marrying age in this time.

"That is the plan," Seth replied. "But I'm not sure if it will happen or not. Your mother's cousin, Prince Saru, is in charge because his father has been ill for years. I don't think he wants to ally himself with Egypt. He isn't outright fighting Egypt at this time, but I don't doubt he is making plans to do so in the future. He isn't strong enough right now to take on the Egyptian army, but if he makes enough other allies, I think he will try. We chose not to stay in the palace because there is just something about that man. I don't trust him."

"What will happen to her if she doesn't go to Egypt?" I asked. My mother's situation was a bit worrisome now. I didn't understand why Logan chose to come back at this exact moment. He had chosen the time after all.

Seth twirled a piece of my hair around his fingers. "More than likely he will marry her off to which ever country he still needs help from. I know both the Hittites and the Assyrians are looking to claim Nahrin. I don't think he is looking to Egypt to help, but he's trying to keep both of them happy for the time being."

My breath caught in my throat. He was telling me the worst thing I could think of. My mother ran away from this time to avoid exactly what was happening. Now she was back in the middle of it. Not keeping secrets was a bit hard. Seth tried to tell me the truth gently, but it still hurt.

"But she's old," I replied before I could help it.

Seth laughed. "Yes, to our time she is old, but since she lived in your time no one here can guess her real age. She looks as young as some of the twenty-year-olds that grew up in this harsher time. She looks older to these people, but not old enough that she wouldn't be able to bear more children."

"I need to help her," I replied, sitting up and looking to the mass of fabric on the floor that was my tunic.

Seth pinned me back to the bed just as quick as I sat up. The sheet was only loosely covering me. Tingles of anticipation tickled through me down to my toes.

"You are going nowhere right now," he replied and began kissing down my neck.

When he was like that, he was right. I wasn't going anywhere at that point. I was his completely.

Seth paused in his kisses. "We don't know what Prince Saru will decide, so we can't make any plans to take your mother until we know. He could still surprise us and let her come with us," Seth explained as he began kissing me again.

"Are your orders to leave her here?" I asked. General Paramessu didn't seem like the type that would take her and potentially start a war.

"My orders are to be as persuasive as I can to get her back to Egypt. Little does my father know that I don't think that prince could be persuaded to do anything." Seth tugged on the covers I was still holding up against me.

"Are you trying to persuade me to do something?" I asked with a smile.

"Yes, is it working?" he asked, winning a few inches with his last tug.

"Seti," Dee called from behind the closed door. Seth sighed and stood up to answer the door. I pulled the sheet up higher.

"Yes?" Seth replied as he opened the door. It wasn't wide open, but I was sure Dee could see inside. Being a gentleman, Dee kept his eyes on Seth.

"Our escorts are here now," Dee explained his intrusion.

"Now?" Seth replied. Obviously, he wasn't expecting them so soon.

"Yes. Downstairs," Dee replied.

"Fine. Can you bring up some extra food and drink for Mari? I'll gather the men and be right down," Seth replied while shutting the door. He straightened out his shendyt and pulled another cloth over his short hair.

"What do I do now?" I asked. He was running off to save my mother, which was meant to be my job, according to my plans.

"Nothing. You sit here and wait," Seth replied. "You're not leave this room. It isn't safe anywhere in this city for you. Dee will bring some food for you to last the day. I will be home by evening at the latest."

How was I to just sit and wait? I wasn't good at waiting. This was my fight. I wanted to be there. I needed to see my mother. Was she okay? Was she being treated well by her family? Or were they are rotten as I pictured, forcing her to run away when she was younger than me? Seth watched my face before coming back over. I was not a fan of just waiting.

"I can't explain this any better to you. For your own safety, you have to stay here. Your hair alone will give away who you are. While most people will let you be, fearing the wrath of the nobles, others might not. You could be an easy way for some to make money— if they find a royal maiden outside the palace. That isn't allowed and you could fetch a nice ransom. Please, just stay here. Don't be seen by anyone," Seth pleaded. I heard the desperation in his voice. "I can't go off and do this if I'm worried about you."

I didn't need to see his eyes to know how concerned he was about me. I wanted to be helping my mother, but Seth was right. I didn't know enough about this place, and would be a hindrance to him more than a help.

"I will," I promised. Seth pulled me up, sheet and all, to kiss me one last time before he left.

CHAPTER 8

FINDING MOM

I waited around all day for Seth to return. I was lucky Dee brought me food like Seth asked or I would have missed lunch by staying in the room. I had the door barred, and there was nothing to do in the small space. There was less space than the dorm room I shared with Sim. I paced for a little bit. I slept for a little bit. I even tried to give myself a bit of a sponge bath from the small bowl of water we had to use. A world without technology was boring, and a world without books was even worse. I didn't want to get stuck in the past without books. I'd have to live somewhere with books. Did they let women be scholars? Then again, that wasn't the kind of book I was looking for. I never did ask Logan if we could take stuff back with us.

I did end up spending the majority of the day sitting in the window. Our room was on the backside of the building, but we had the corner room. From the angle of the window I could see a small patch of the street. I wasn't allowed to look around the day before, but I could now in my hidden perch. I wasn't disobeying Seth since I kept my hair covered. If someone even caught the sliver of me in the window, they wouldn't know who I was.

By nightfall my stomach was growling again. Breakfast before dawn, and a lunch on my own, wasn't enough to fill me by the time the sky turned black. I sat in complete darkness as the sun faded away. Because I wasn't sure how to light the candles in the room. Luckily enough I did figure out how to get my billowy tunic back on, therefore I wasn't naked. I jumped at the sound of the door handle being turned, even though I knew it wouldn't open.

"Mari," Seth said quietly.

I hurried to the door and opened it. Seth was carrying more food as he entered. I shut the door behind him and waited for Seth to set the tray down. I didn't even care what it was this time, I was too hungry. Hot food smelled delicious to me. I wasn't cut out for his time period and the lack of nutrition. Seth set the tray on the bed and the burning candle he brought with him onto the bare nightstand. He used the candle to light the lamp that I had no idea how to use. I felt helpless in this new time.

"What happened?" I asked.

"Eat first," Seth ordered. He handed me a dish of something but took none for himself.

I shoveled the mush and chunks of who knows what into my mouth and stared at him. He took one of the glasses. I couldn't tell by the dim light in the room, but I was pretty sure it wasn't water. Seth stood by the window and looked outside as I ate in silence. When the food was finally gone, I waited for him. He didn't say anything or turn around. I stood up and walked over to him. I placed a hand on his shoulder. He covered it with his own larger hand.

"Prince Saru has agreed to the Hittite King's request of your mother," Seth told me.

"What does that mean?" I asked.

"In three days, your mother will be shipped north to marry the Hittite king as his twelfth wife," Seth answered.

I sat back down on the bed. That wasn't supposed to

happen. My mother was meant to be happy in the past. The goddess sent her back. She said my mother belonged here. My mother didn't belong in a place that traded her like cattle. She was a person, not an object. Why couldn't these men see it that way?

"What can we do?" I asked as Seth sat beside me.

"I don't know, Mari," Seth replied while putting his arms around me. "I really don't know."

That was answer enough for my earlier question. The general hadn't agreed to Seth taking my mother back by force. I had no doubt that Seth's order was for him to return back to the military with or without my mother. General Paramessu was a smart general, and not one who would place such a risk on his country or his son. I hated, but respected, that.

"It's not fair," I said, trying to hold more tears at bay. I had cried enough over and for my mother. "She ran away from a life of being sent off as a bargaining chip between nations. The goddess even helped her. But where is the goddess now? Why is my mother being forced to live the life she tried hard to avoid? We have to do something."

"I know," Seth replied, pulling me to his chest. "I know. Just give me some time. We'll think of something."

I sniffled and cuddled into his arms. We had to think of something, and we had three days. I looked down at my arm. The lines were almost full again. I would be able to travel with her, but now I was unsure how to even do that. I was nowhere near her, and Seth didn't want me near the palace because of who I was. I was stuck.

Seth picked up my arm and looked at the lines. He turned my arm around and traced the lines with his finger. He was as amazed by them as I was.

"They really are growing, aren't they?" he said.

He had seen the lines the day before, but they weren't much beyond a single swirl around my wrist and few up my arm. If I hadn't let go of Logan, they would have been full and ready to travel like we had planned. Oh well. I enjoyed my time letting them grow back. They now stretched up my forearm.

"They still have a little to go, and then I can travel again," I replied. Seth nodded and traced the lines with his fingers back down to where they started.

"This will take some getting used to," Seth replied, looking closer at them.

"For you, but not anyone else. Only people who have time traveled before can see them," I explained. "They're almost full. That means I can travel and take someone back with me. If I can get close to my mother, I can take her back," I added before Seth could change the subject off my mother completely.

"No," Seth replied. "I'll talk with Dee. We will find a way that doesn't involve putting you in the middle of it. I need you safe. I have no idea what I'd do without you, or if you got hurt."

"But I'll be safe. See the lines? They prove it. If I get stuck, then I can just travel away," I explained. "Superhero powers. Trust me. I can do this."

"No," Seth said with more finality to his voice. "I'm not letting you go off and potentially get taken away from me. These last six months have been torture, never knowing when I'd see you again. If you step foot in the palace, they will keep you from me, whether you want to be with me or not. I'm only a soldier. Royalty marries other royalty. I can't have that, time travel or not."

I couldn't agree with his assessment that my new traveling abilities wouldn't help, but I could agree that it was torture. And I didn't want to torment him, he deserved that much.

"But I thought your father agreed to us being married," I replied. "They would have never accepted that."

"Well sometimes they are forced to accept marriages," Seth cryptically replied, looking back to the window and not meeting my eyes.

"How?" I asked. I was a bit suspicious, but more than that, was wondering if he knew something that could help my mother.

"If you were with child," he replied.

"But that didn't work for my mother," I answered, completely glazing over the fact that he admitted his father wanted him to knock me up that day they found me.

"Because she was still here and promised to someone else. If you were with my people, and protected by them, your cousin would have no choice but agree to the marriage or disown you. Your mother's problem was that no one would have protected her. Her own people wouldn't have wanted you born, and my people would have seen it as a sin to dirty the pharaoh's future wife. You wouldn't be in the same position with me. My father would protect us, and I would protect you."

"This world is messed up," I added, and shook my head. Love was love, and no one could control who they fell for.

"Don't worry about your mother. Let me do this. Let me save your mother. Let me protect you," Seth begged. I couldn't say no to that.

I cuddled close to him as he dimmed the light in the room. Everything was so messed up, and it was all my fault. The wheels turned in Seth's head. He was planning something, but he didn't realize that putting himself in danger was also torture to me. He wanted to protect me, and I wanted to protect him. I wouldn't be able to stand by and watch him get hurt. This time period was dangerous, and I was sure he was planning something risky. As much as he wanted to keep me safe, I wanted the exact same for him.

The next two days were slow for me, but quick for Seth. Dee came by each morning and tried to come up with ways of getting to my mother. There was nothing they could agree on and nothing really seemed feasible actually. My mother was left in the palace, preparing to go off to be a wife to a man she didn't love. It wasn't fair.

By afternoon, the guys both left me alone as they scouted out the city. They were trying to find a way as best they could, but it was failing. They didn't have many options since they weren't in their own country, and my mother was heavily guarded. After her last disappearance, it seemed that the Nahrin weren't taking any chances this time.

When the third day came, the last full day my mother would be in the city, I had to take things into my own hands. Seth was trying his hardest. He wanted me to stay in his room all day and be safe, but she was still my mother. I had listened to the guys plan and throw out options. They were nowhere close to saving her. There would be a dinner tonight, and she would be given away first thing in the morning. Time was running out, and they couldn't stop my mother's fate. I trusted Seth to try his hardest no matter what, and knew he would do everything in his power to save my mother, but sometimes trying hard wasn't enough. Sometimes it took more than you could give. Sometimes, someone else had to help.

I waited until the guys were gone out into the city again before I made my move. I couldn't delay any longer as she was soon to be moved out of the city. I had no clue where to find her beyond the fact that she was in the large palace not too far away. If they took her, it would be even harder for me to find her, and you never knew what could happen on the way. It seemed like it wasn't uncommon to kidnap a princess, I learned this after I listening to Seth and Dee throw out ideas. They could be ransomed for large amounts to various countries. If she left now, it might be close to impossible to ever find her again. I had to try to rescue her. I could send her home and come right back to the room where Dee and Seth would be waiting for me. We'd need to leave quickly since the Egyptians would be the first people they would blame for her disappearance, but that's where Logan would come in. I tried several time to tell Seth of my plan, but he wouldn't listen. He refused to allow me near my mother. I checked the door lock a second time before speaking. My plan was solid, and this time I wasn't going to deviate from it.

"Logan," I called. He said he would be watching me. I hoped that was true.

Logan appeared before me. It was strange to see him dressed in the rich tunics of the wealthier men around the city, as I had grown accustomed to seeing Dee and Seth in barely anything. Relief lined Logan's face.

"Thank the goddess you called for me," Logan said, coming over and inspecting me. "I have been looking all around the city for days, but couldn't find you."

"I've kind of been here for days," I added, motioning around the room.

"That was a very smart decision. They would have hauled you off to the palace by now if anyone knew you were here," Logan commented. "How'd you get into a room like this?" I had no money either, so it would seem strange.

"It's Seth's room," I replied before I realized that maybe his wasn't the best name to mention. Anger flashed briefly across Logan's face before he was back to normal. I don't think he thought I saw it, but I did. My being with Seth angered him. Maybe calling to him was a bad idea after all.

"And yet you call for me," he commented, his cocky self easily returning.

"I need help," I said, only further boosting his

arrogance that I'd come to him over Seth. "I want to get into the palace to take my mother home like we planned. Seth doesn't think it is safe for me to be there."

"It isn't, but didn't you tell him about being able to time travel?" Logan replied. He wasn't immediately telling me *no* like Seth had.

"Yes, but Seth still doesn't think it's safe. I just need to get in and get close to my mom. I have to save her. I can't let her be sold off to the highest bidder. She's my mom," I explained. "Once I get her home, I will come right back here for Seth and Dee. We can take them home also."

"The plan is your mother, and then get the guys out right away?" Logan asked.

"Yes, can you help me get to her, and then come back and tell the guys what the plan is?" I asked. I would have left Seth a note if they had a pen and paper in the room. One more thing for my list of things the past was annoying about.

"Yes, but what will you do then?" Logan replied. "You need a stone to send her into the future."

"Which you have, right?" I asked, not giving away the second line on my arm. I had a feeling from his look not even moments ago, that he would not come back for Seth if he had the choice.

"I don't have it on me," he replied. "I'll have to go get it, and some sort of disguise that will allow you to get close to your mother."

"Fine, but come right back. I don't know how long Seth will be out with Dee," I replied. Logan was already fading away. He wasn't gone for more than two seconds before he returned with clothing that he handed to me.

I took the lighter dress and over tunic. I indicated to Logan to turn around. I wasn't dressing in front of him, friends or not. Logan complied, but gave me a suggestive smile first. *That was exactly why.*

I got the clothing on quickly with my back turned to

Logan. While I was completely comfortable with Seth in the small room, I wasn't with Logan. He still made me wonder about his motives. He was doing exactly what I asked, but I still was unsure. Something just didn't seem right. He didn't even try to bargain, or ask for something in return.

"Now we need to fix your hair, too," Logan said, stepping closer with something in his hand. He had something dark-colored and stinky. I didn't ask what, and got the hint at what he was going to do. I stood still as he applied the powdery substance to my hair. There was no mirror in the room, but Logan was happy with the results.

"Then you'll take me to her? This sounds like a good plan?" I asked.

Logan hadn't tried to talk me out of anything like Seth did. It was strange. I knew Seth's intentions were to keep me safe, but Logan was a mystery. He claimed to still love me and want to help me, but had no objections to what I suggested. Maybe Seth was just being overprotective and Logan was not. Maybe my plan was exactly what we needed to do. I couldn't be sure, and I couldn't read Logan's face.

"I promised Ty that I'd help you, and I don't break promises. I can take you inside the palace, as close to your mom as I can get. You'll have to do the rest. There are female servants all over the women's wing. You should fit in fine. Just find your mom and get out of there as fast as you can," Logan said, offering me his arm.

"And then you'll get Seth and Dee out of here?" I added the second part of my plan.

"Yes, I'll get them both home as soon as I see your mother there," Logan answered.

I took his arm, and we immediately were inside a building. Logan disappeared as quickly as he had appeared, and I was left alone. I didn't even look around much as I moved quietly down the empty hallway to a place where I heard talking. As I neared a corner, I looked around it carefully. Beautiful arches led into an open courtyard. Women and children of all ages were sitting or running around. There was a pool or fountain of some sort in the middle of the open-roofed room, and several children were playing in it no matter what the mothers yelled to them. Plants grew around the courtyard, and the scent of flowers came from the slight breeze. Outside the arches, just down the hallway from me, were several soldiers walking around with swords hanging from their belts. There was no way I was going to be able to walk by them and not be noticed.

I hid back around my corner. My mother had to be in there somewhere. It was almost like how I could feel Seth; I could feel her now, too. I had the same sort of tingles in my arm, but this time instead of excitement, which was always with Seth's, I felt more at peace, more like love coming from the carnelian and chrysoprase lines. She was in that room, but so were at least six dozen other people, too. And they were guarded, whether to keep people out or in, it wasn't a good situation for me. I heard walking down the hallway from behind the guards and snuck another peek. Two women dressed like me entered the open courtyard. Maybe they would just allow me in. I waited a few more minutes because I still wasn't sure. I needed to see more people enter dressed like me. I needed to do exactly what they did.

Leaning against the wall, I tried to decide what to do. I could just walk past the guards and pretend I was there for a reason, but I was unsure what the women were even doing who were coming in and out of the courtyard. I'd need to know more.

I looked around the corner again to see two more women walking past the guards. It looked easy enough, but that wasn't necessarily a good sign. They were all going in pairs of two. Unless I found someone to go with,

I would stick out. I glanced around the courtyard. It was enormous, and I wasn't sure where my mother was in the gaggle of women. I pulled back to think more about what to do when I caught a flash of fabric coming around the corner behind me. Someone appeared and squealed at my presence there.

I didn't even think, but just time traveled between my location and into the courtyard. I ended up in the dark corner that I had been thinking would be a good hiding spot once I was able to get there, but I didn't intend to just travel there. Most of the women looked to the open arches toward the squealing woman that entered through it. I couldn't see a single face to look for my mother. The guards had yelled for backup and more men arrived. They stood just outside the arches as the woman calmed down and finally talked to the guards. The room went back into their normal chatter.

The distraction, which I unintentionally caused, gave me time to look around the courtyard from a new perspective. A group of younger women sat the closest to me. I saw all their faces and knew none were my mother. The rest were more confusing as I couldn't see their faces well enough to even guess which one was my mother. Most of the women had a dark brown color for their hair, but many others had the same red sheen to their brown hair as my mother did. I could see now how Seth said I'd be considered family to these people that I knew nothing about. Several of the women from my view could be my mother, but I wasn't sure.

"What are you doing here?" a shrill voice asked me from behind. I guess my hiding spot wasn't as good as I thought.

"Nothing, miss," I replied, trying to be the dutiful servant. "I'm new here." I hoped that would be enough of an explanation.

"Where is your trainer, then?" the woman asked,

eyeing me over. With the commotion and me being alone, I kind of stuck out like a sore thumb.

"They just left me here to wait for them to return," I replied. It did seem like a good explanation.

"Then I guess I'll wait with you," the lady suggested, not believing me. I now saw exactly how this plan wouldn't work. Even though the women sat around and didn't seem to notice the working women that came and went, that wasn't the case.

"Who are you working for?" the lady asked casually.

I didn't understand the question. Did she think I was a spy?

"Which lady were you assigned to?" the lady repeated more slowly, like I was dim-witted and didn't understand her question.

"Hepa," I spat out. My mother was the only one I knew, and if I said her, maybe this lady would direct me to my mother.

"Hepa?" the lady questioned, raising her eyebrows.

"Yes," I squeaked and looked back at the floor. I needed this lady to believe me.

"In that case, we should wait with Lady Saska," the lady replied with a smile that was not friendly in the least, and I didn't understand why. There was some joke to her words that I didn't get.

The lady moved around the edge of the courtyard, and I followed. I had to hope she would lead me right to my mother, and this Lady Saska would be with her. As we made it to the edge nearest the columns that led out, I still didn't see my mother anywhere. I continued to gaze about and barely stopped in time to not step on the lady's clothing in front of me. I hadn't notice her stopping.

I looked up in time to see we were right next to the lady that had been squealing for the guards earlier. She was the one that saw me spying into the courtyard. This wasn't good. I needed to get out right away, but noticed that the tips of the lines on my arm were faded. When I jumped into the courtyard, I did it out of instinct and used up some of my time traveling. I'd have to wait to do it again. I was stuck, and my mother was nowhere in sight.

"Lady Saska," the woman who had been leading me called to the ornately decorated woman.

Lady Saska was inches taller than the rest of the women and had hair that was a rich chocolate brown. It cascaded in curls down her back and not a strand looked out of place. I could tell now that I was closer, she was the most ornately dressed of all the women, and had jewelry dripping off every place you could put it. Her hair had jewels, her throat had multiple necklaces on it, her wrists chimed with every movement due to the amount of bracelets. Even her dress had stones sewn into it.

Lady Saska turned to the voice of the woman who spoke.

"I found this trash hiding around the back. I thought maybe she was the one you were looking for," the lady replied.

I sucked in a breath. I had been caught and not even realized it. I had walked right into this trap. I was unsure now that my mother was really around these women. I let my instincts kick in and messed up again.

Lady Saska turned her icy blue eyes on me. She scowled and looked closer at me.

"Yes, she looks about the right height," Lady Saska replied. "Guards," she called to the men standing just outside the columns. "Take this servant away to be punished."

Two men stepped only feet into the open room. They grabbed my arms roughly and pinned them behind me. I didn't struggle as I had no clue what was going on. I could leave soon, anyway.

"Yes, my lady," one of the guards replied. "How would you like to be her punishment?"

"Ten lashings should do, and then make sure she spends a week down in the dungeon," Lady Saska replied. "We can never be too safe in these difficult times. She might be a spy."

"I'm no spy," I answered before one of the guards hit me across the face. My lip cut on one of my teeth and blood pooled in my mouth.

"Only royalty can address our future queen," the guard huffed. Lady Saska smiled sweetly at the man, like he had just protected her honor.

"I'm no spy," I repeated, this time to the guard. I stared at his eyes, challenging him to hit me again. I didn't address their future queen, but I was sure she had heard me.

"I think she was sent here to take Lady Hepa away," the lady who found me told Saska.

Saska's smile temporarily fell at my mother's name. She looked at me and glared. "I take that back. This one has to be a spy. Lash her until she tells you who she is working for." Her voice was laced with anger. I thought maybe this lady was really trying to protect her women, but now something broke through her perfect exterior. My arm tingled with that feeling of love again, and I knew my mother was nearby.

"Hepa is my mother," I declared. I still felt like my mother was around somewhere. I couldn't see her, but she was there.

I needed to stall the men from taking me away to be able to see her. My travel powers would be back soon, and I would free her. The Lady Saska that stood before me was no one that I wanted my mom left around. My mother was a kind, gentle soul. There was nothing kind in this woman even if what she called me could be true, in a way. Perhaps I was a spy after all. My plans were to free my mother, but I'd never admit that. The women had stopped their talking and all stared at us as we spoke with the guards. Now they all whispered between them.

"Impossible," Lady Saska replied. "I see we need more punishments to teach her not to lie." Lady Saska tapped her lips as she thought.

"My mother is Hepa," I repeated as some of the whispers grew louder. Many of the women seemed to think I looked like her.

"Hepa has no children," Lady Saska repeated, like saying it would make it so. Maybe in her book it did. "Send her to the guard's quarters first. Maybe you guys can convince her to tell the truth, and if not, then you can just have some fun with her."

My mouth dropped. This lady was truly evil.

The warm tingles in my arms increased. My mother was around somewhere close.

"Mom," I yelled over the murmur of the women. They seemed to be just as shocked as I was. "Mom," I yelled again, as loud as I could.

The guards weren't waiting for Lady Saska to order us away. They had already begun to drag me out of the women's courtyard. This time I struggled. My mother was near. Someone pushed aside women in the crowd that were all standing and watching me. The person came closer, and I smiled in relief. I had found her. It was my mother.

CHAPTER 9

A WORLD I WANTED TO AVOID

"**Mari?**" **My mother** asked, looking at me closely. I'm sure the hair threw her for a loop. It stunk, too.

"Mom," I replied, trying to pull my arms from the guards. They were not letting go.

"Release the girl," a regal lady said from behind my mother. She had followed my mother through the crowd.

"Our orders," one of the guards complained. He seemed the most eager to drag me away.

"Are not my orders, and I'm the one in charge," the older lady with my mother said to the two guards. They let go as they were reminded. Lady Saska didn't look too pleased with either being upstaged by the older lady, or that I truly was my mother's child, maybe both.

My mother ran over and hugged me. It was strange to see her made up in the same garb as the rest of the women, long tunics that were embroidered, and in the case of Lady Saska, covered in jewels of various colors. My mother looked out of place not being in her normal business skirts that were all in various dull colors. This time seemed too colorful for my mother. My mom pulled me away from Lady Saska and her friend, and down to the other regal lady of the room.

"You can't just take her word on that," Lady Saska complained while the guards left. "You know Hepa would lie to save a slave. This is a matter that must be determined by my husband." Lady Saska's hands were on her hips as she complained like a spoiled child.

"You forget that as long as my husband is alive, this is my part of the palace. You are merely a guest here, Lady Saska. You may be the mother to my grandchildren, but you are still a princess. I am a queen. It would do you well to remember that before deciding how anyone is punished. I might just decide you should have the same punishment to learn a lesson," the older lady replied, turning to me.

Lady Saska turned a bright shade of red either from embarrassment or anger. I had a feeling that girl was used getting her way. She huffed a little as she stood in her place, and the older lady ignored her. I wanted to laugh at the jeweled lady's little fit. It was rather comical.

The older lady looked at me. Stepping closer, she gently took my face in her hands. She turned my face left and then right as she studied me before looking to my mother.

"I don't doubt this child is Hepa's," the older lady said. "Now let's go get her cleaned up before we present her to Prince Saru." Lady Saska glared at me in anger now. I had a feeling she already knew that I was my mother's child, and was trying to punish me anyways.

My mother wrapped her arm around me as we followed behind the older lady. The crowd parted for us as we walked further into the courtyard. Women stared and some whispered. It looked like I was the new bit of gossip. When we were sufficiently away from the groups of women, who were slowly going back to their spots around the room, the older lady spoke.

"Dear child, what were you doing sneaking in the palace? Hepa said you were safely away," she told me.

"Didn't Hepa tell you to stay away from here?"

I looked at my mom, and then the older lady. My mother never told me anything, and I sure didn't know that I was to stay away. My mom shrugged and I was unsure what game we were playing now. Did my mother tell anyone the real truth? What was the lie she told? What should I say or not say?

"This is my aunt, Queen Juni," my mom explained, interrupting the questions I was asking myself.

"Why would she tell me to stay away from here?" I asked, looking to my mom.

My mom looked to her aunt and shook her head no. My aunt shook her head back. There was an answer there, I was sure of it. They weren't telling me something.

"This, my dear, is our bathing room. We need to get you cleaned up and that muck out of your hair before you see my son. Once your red hair is present, Saska will not be able to deny that you are Hepa's child," Aunt Juni explained. She had seen through my disguise.

I looked at the large pool she referred to as a bath. It wasn't a bath, exactly, it was a swimming pool, maybe even Olympic-sized. There were attendants standing alongside one of the walls holding various objects like towels or bottles I assumed had soap, but otherwise there was no one in the water. I looked over to my mother. It was ridiculous to call it a bath. It was skinny dipping if you asked me.

"The water is warm," my mother told me.

I looked back at the water. It seemed a little excessive to me.

"And you don't just have a tub-sized version of this?" I asked my mother. She smiled and shook her head. I nodded. Of course they didn't. I went from using a bowl to a swimming pool to clean myself. I had a feeling my life would be ever changing like this.

"I'll help you get that stuff out of your hair," she

offered.

I stripped out of my clothing and hopped in the water quickly. I was warm for being in such a large body of water. I had expected it only to be lukewarm. I dunked my head under the water and watched it turn the water a black color. When I came back up, I made my way over to my mother at the edge. I pulled my head far enough out of the water that she could kneel on the side while she used some sort of soaps in my hair. I silently sat there while she scrubbed my hair clean. I waited for her to say something, but she said nothing. By the time my hair was clean, I was turning into a prune from being in the water too long. I climbed out to be wrapped in a towel before being taken to a lounging chair near the water. The servants were working at rubbing some sort of perfumed oil into my skin while trying their best to dry my thick hair. When they finally finished, I did feel refreshed and clean, but the smell of the oils was a bit much for me. I wasn't one to even use perfumes daily, but I couldn't complain. It was good to get the dirt off me.

Sometime during my bath, my clothes disappeared and so did Aunt Juni. My mother led me back through the halls, near the courtyard that all the women were in. Instead of entering the courtyard, she led me down an adjacent hallway to a bedroom. She picked out a dress and handed it to me.

"What are you doing here?" she finally asked as she shut the door and seemed sure we wouldn't be overheard.

"I came to get you," I replied, just as quietly. I had no clue what was safe and what wasn't in the place.

"Oh, honey." My mother bumped her forehead to mine. "You can't save me. This is my life." She stated it like it was obvious that her fate was already determined. I hated when my mother sat back and let life pass her by like that. I knew where I got my fight to change everything from- it had to be my father.

"It doesn't have to be," I replied. I needed her to see the truth. "I'll take you back with me."

"For how long?" She sighed, wrapping her arms around me like I was a little kid again. "Eventually I have to be here. This is where I was born, and this is where I will die," she replied, just as the goddess told me. She had accepted her fate.

"Why?" I asked, pulling back from her and finally started to get dressed in the clothing that was lying out. I needed away from her comforting hugs. She was trying her best to hug me into acceptance of her fate. "Why does it have to be that way?"

"Because that's how it works. We can't change time," my mom replied. "The goddess gave me way more than I ever expected to get. I got nineteen years with you. I got to watch you grow up. You've turned into a beautiful woman. But I need you to leave after meeting Prince Saru. You can't stay here."

"I'm not leaving without you," I replied stubbornly. And I wasn't. She was going to married off to a man with eleven wives. I was saving her.

"You can't take me with you. I no longer have the goddess stone," my mom explained, blowing off my stubbornness. That's when it hit me. Logan never gave me Ty's stone. It didn't matter completely because I could always get my mother home with the stones on my arm, but I did find it strange. Either he was setting me up to fail, or he had noticed the chrysoprase on my arm.

"But I do," I replied and pointed to my arm. My mom squinted in the dim light and pulled my arm closer to the only window in the room.

"What is this?" she asked. She never was a fan of tattoos. I kind of wanted to tease and tell her it was a college rebellion thing, but we had limited time.

"Those are a blessed carnelian and chrysoprase in my arms. They work just like if they were whole stones. I can

157

use them to go through time, Mom. I can save you. If you look here," I pointed to the lines that ended at my forearm, "there is a little missing. Once it's full and comes to a point, I can travel anywhere in time. I can take you home. I have two stones. Please let me save you."

My mom smiled, but it wasn't a happy smile. It was a patronizing smile, and I knew what she was going to say. She had believed and trusted the goddess completely. My mother wouldn't go willingly to the future.

"Honey, this was always meant to be my destiny. I was born to be a pawn by being female," she replied. "Use your stones to get free of here. Live the life I wanted for you. Please don't make me watch you become subjected to the same fate I have been. Go, live, find love, be happy."

"I can't leave you here unhappy," I replied. "If you won't leave to come the future, let me take you to Dad. Tell me who he is and I'll take you to him."

My mom rearranged my clothing and hugged me close.

"I can't let you do that either," she responded. "I'm in the same spot I was years ago. I have already been given to someone else. If you take me to your father, a non-royal, then my cousin will be mad. I can't bring that upon your father now. Besides, I don't even know if he's alive in this time. He was part of the military. They tend to not have a long life."

"I'm not leaving you here," I added obstinately. It didn't matter what she said. She was coming home with me. I didn't find her living happily in the past, which meant she was going to the future.

"I know that. You're as stubborn as your father. You didn't get that from me," she answered, shaking her head. I was driving her as nuts as she was driving me.

The door to the room opened and Aunt Juni walked in. Several maids dressed the way I was before entered with her. I now got the whole *who are you assigned to* thing. Funny how no one was assigned to my mother. I had to wonder what that meant.

"My son would like to see you both," Aunt Juni told me as she shared a look with my mother.

"What?" I asked. Something was up. They kept talking with just their eyes.

My aunt shook her head, indicating the women standing right behind her. No wonder my mother was quiet while bathing me. While I didn't really notice the servants, they must have been noticing us. It seemed I had a bit to learn about this family I never knew.

I followed my great aunt out of my mother's room and the women's courtyard. After leaving the entrance hallway I already had seen, we moved further into the palace. Soon we entered a large room with extensive artwork on the walls. Drawings and tiles lined every open space, from the bottom to the top of the walls. People milled about the large room, as if waiting for something.

My aunt paused after we entered. She was looking around and saw something. I noticed what she was looking at. Lady Saska was across the room with a bearded man that wasn't quite as tall as her. He wore as many jewels as Lady Saska did. I kind of got the feeling they were a matched pair. And if that was true, it didn't bode well for me. I had guessed that Lady Saska might be the wife of my mother's cousin, but the people standing there now basically confirmed what I expected. When Lady Saska finally noticed us, her cheerful smile immediately disappeared and her face turned to disgust. The man with her noticed us and abruptly turned. He followed the narrower hallway at the back of the hall, past the ten-foot-tall statues. I had no idea what animal they were.

Aunt Juni took the man's move as a lead to follow. My mother looped her arm in mine and led us behind her aunt. People in the room talked amongst themselves, yet many snuck glances at my mother and me. I wondered if my mother's new husband was in the room. Everyone looked like they were elites.

"No matter what happens, don't speak unless I say it's okay. Follow my lead," my mother whispered in my ear. "And don't mention that your father is Egyptian."

As we passed the large statues my mother straightened up, like she was preparing for a battle. We rounded the corner, and I saw the battlefield. There were two large thrones sitting at the end of the smaller attached room. Lady Saska was sitting in one and the man with her was in the other. He was no doubt my mother's cousin, Prince Saru.

Prince Saru watched us intently as we walked through the empty room to him. His gaze was like a hawk flying above, surveying the scene. He was examining every detail of me before turning to his mother. With one look, he had made a decision.

Aunt Juni walked up to the throne and stiffly kissed his forehead beneath his brown curls. I stayed back with my mother. When she bowed at the waist, I did the same. I waited until she brought her head up before I followed.

"Cousin Hepa, you failed to mention you had a child," Prince Saru began by scolding my mother.

Aunt Juni stood beside us, and replied before my mother could.

"Really? I knew," she replied.

"And you failed to tell me?" Prince Saru replied.

Aunt Juni casually shrugged. "It must have slipped my mind. I'm getting older after all."

I was sure that wasn't the case.

"You vouch for her, Mother?" Prince Saru asked suspiciously. He didn't believe his mother had forgotten either, but he didn't seem to want to call her out on it.

"I wouldn't be here now if I didn't," Aunt Juni replied. "Besides, you'd have to be blind to not see the resemblance, even if she were disguised. Everything about her, except for her eyes, is her mother's." I liked how she threw in a dig at her evil daughter-in-law. I got the feeling there was no love between the queen and her princess daughter-in-law.

Prince Saru stood and walked down the two steps to where we were standing. He stopped right in front of me, and I kept my gaze steady, straight ahead. Prince Saru walked around me to view me from every angle. He returned in front of me and lifted my face to look into my eyes. His grip was pinching me, but I refused to show that it hurt. He nodded as if he were answering his own question in his head.

"Who is your father?" he asked.

"I have no idea," I replied. I had a feeling that honesty was the best policy with this man.

"Where have you been living?"

"With a man I thought was my grandfather. I just found out he wasn't," I answered.

Prince Saru let go of my face and walked back up to the throne. He sat down with some elegance and lots of arrogance. He took his time getting comfortable, and we all waited and watched him. He liked to be the center of attention. His wife waited eagerly beside him and was much less patient.

"She's telling the truth," he said to his wife, though we could hear him also.

"But, but..." Lady Saska began to argue, her eagerness turning to anger as she sputtered.

"Who is her father?" Prince Saru asked my mother.

"I don't know," my mother replied. Prince Saru nodded. He didn't seem upset that he thought he had been lied to.

I knew that was a lie, but it didn't seem that Prince Saru could read her as easily as me. I had a bit to learn about this world my mother lived in.

"How old is she?" he asked my mother. I no longer existed in the conversation.

"Nineteen," my mom replied.

"Impossible," Lady Saska replied. I looked at her and had no idea why she would care. "She only looks fifteen."

"And I only look to be in my mid-twenties," my mom replied. "Life has been kind to us."

And not you, I wanted to reply. Lady Saska looked much older than my mother, but I got the feeling now that she was actually younger.

"So it has. We will be telling suitors that she is fifteen," Prince Saru replied.

"Suitors?" I asked, and then quickly covered my mouth. I wasn't to talk.

"Yes, suitors," Prince Saru said. "As a royal you will be expected to marry soon. You should have been married already by your age, but I assume by you coming here that means that you are not. I have several allies that are in need of an extra wife. You'd be a suitable trade for protection."

Lady Saska's unhappy face returned to its smile. She seemed to like the idea of me being married off.

"I have several dignitaries here today. We'll announce at Hepa's farewell dinner that I'm looking for a husband for you," Prince Saru replied. Prince Saru looked at me, but his eyes said he was far away in thought. "Yes, this will work quite well." Prince Saru said to himself. He stood up and began to walk away without another word. His wife stood and trailed after him like a puppy looking for attention.

Aunt Juni nodded to my mother, who took my hand and led me back through the small hall and into the larger room. Prince Saru was already talking to one group of men that were lounging around the bigger room. The men looked up at me as I passed. All three of the older bearded men smiled. My mother kept walking and didn't stop until we were back in her room.

Aunt Juni stuck her head in the doorway, where her

maids couldn't hear her as she whispered. "Get this child out of here before tomorrow. He will have her promised to someone by then."

My mom nodded and shut her room door.

"You need to leave now," my mother told me.

"I won't leave without you," I replied. I wasn't backing down on that argument.

"Fine, then I'll leave with you," she told me. I had won. My mother would do anything for me, and I knew it. Maybe it wasn't fair to play her like that, but I needed her back in the future. She was my mother after all.

I looked down at my hand. The lines would soon be complete. We both would be able to leave. I just needed to make sure Logan was ready with the guys.

"Logan," I called quietly.

Logan appeared in the room.

"Mrs. Navina," he said to my mother.

My mother stared at my ex-boyfriend. His sandy blond hair and boyish smile were exactly the same as when he dated me, no matter the clothing he now wore. She had to be shocked to see him.

"Turns out he is Mr. Sangre's biological son," I told my mom to keep her from asking anything more.

My mom just nodded. That was enough for her.

"Logan, we need to get out of here tonight," I told him. "I kind of had to use my travel to not get caught earlier. I can't leave now, but it should be fine tonight. We need to leave then. Will the guys be ready?"

"Yes, tonight it will be," Logan replied.

My mother looked between us.

"Logan is helping us escape, and making sure that everyone is safe," I told her. "He can travel and take people with him. We just need to find a time to sneak away tonight when no one will notice we are gone."

"There is a dinner tonight we need to attend. It will be full of drunk people by the end. We could leave then, and they won't notice we're gone for hours," my mother added.

"That sounds good. When you find a moment alone, I'll come and take her first, and then come back for the guys," Logan replied. He had obviously realized he didn't leave me the stone. I nodded to Logan, and he disappeared.

We stayed in my mother's room until dinnertime. She didn't want me around the other women, and she surely really didn't want me talking to them. Her world was much more complicated than I ever knew. By the time dinner arrived my lines were fully charged, and I could travel at any moment, yet I still didn't trust Logan. I wanted him to take my mom and Dee, and then I'd be gone with Seth before he returned.

When it was time to get ready, although I had already dressed for the day, my mother explained it wouldn't be enough. She got us ready for the dinner. My mother had a chest full of elaborate dresses. We were about the same size, so it was easy to find something in her collection for me. After dresses, she decked us out with jewels on our arms, ears, hair, and even our feet, which wouldn't be seen under the long dresses we wore.

When we finished, Aunt Juni came in with more jewelry than my mom had already put on the both of us, and hair dressers to give us both the same hair styles. It looked like she was doing her best to continue to play up our relationship. She didn't speak beyond telling people what to do the whole time, but her eyes gave away that she knew more. It seemed like she wanted to say more, but she was never alone to be able to do so. I was unsure if it was her son or her daughter-in-law's doing, but Aunt Juni was as trapped as my mother. I felt bad for my elder aunt. This wasn't a world for women. When everything was deemed ready, Aunt Juni left us alone to be summoned to the party.

Aunt Juni paused by me before she left the room. "Take care of her," she told me. She already guessed we were making plans to leave. I wondered how much my mother had told her, but it wasn't like I could ask.

I sat down beside my mother on her bed while we waited. It was already dark outside, and I was ready to get this ridiculous dinner over with and take my mother home.

"I'm sorry I didn't tell you any of this," my mother said.

"I don't think I would have believed you," I replied, which made her smile. It was true. If my mother told me she was royalty from thousands of years before the twenty-first century, I would have laughed. Then I would have asked her to see a shrink. What we were doing now seemed beyond surreal. There was nothing to be sorry about.

"I should have at least told you more about your father," my mom added. That much I would have liked to have known.

"When we get home, we'll have plenty of time for that. You can tell me everything," I said. My mom smiled and nodded.

"You're so much like him. I'm glad that you inherited your father's logic also." She put her arm around me, and we leaned our heads together.

"But I got your heart." I snuggled into her arm. It was true. Even though at times I thought I was the exact opposite of her, I did have her compassion.

She kept her arms around me as we waited. No matter what time, or where we had to go, she was my mother and always would be. I watched lady after lady be escorted past our room and got the feeling we would be last. That was okay, though. I was happy where we were. It had been years since we had sat alone for so long. I was always a momma's girl as a child, but once I was a teen I was never home, or she was too busy. We rarely had time anymore to eat a meal before we had to get to our obligations. I kind of missed being a child. Now, sitting beside her brought back all the memories. My mother was a great mom. The fact that she ran away from this world to give me a good life alone made her world's best mom, and even now she was trying to protect me from it.

"If you could do anything, and live in any time, what would you do?" I asked.

My mom smiled. "I'd find your father. I know he's probably married with children by now, if he's still alive, but I'm sure he would still love me. You only find true love like that once a life time. You'll know it someday."

I nodded along with her. That was Seth to me, a once-in-a-lifetime find. I hated to think of him now, and how worried he would be, but I couldn't help but smile as I did. Just picturing Seth made me smile. My mother noticed.

"You found yours, didn't you?" my mom said. I wasn't going to say anything more to complicate matters. I just nodded. "Is he cute?"

"Yes," I replied.

"Is he available? Going after people with girlfriends never works," my mom added. I almost laughed. It was just like my mom to sit here giving me love advice as we were on our way to a dinner where I was to be auctioned off to the highest bidder.

"Not anymore," I replied.

"Aww, honey. I wish I could meet this guy right now. You'll have to bring him home to your grandfather's for dinner when we get back," she added. I liked that she was already making plans for the future. I thought I'd have to force her to return.

166

I didn't know if I should tell her the truth about Seth. She didn't ask about Logan bringing more people to the future, but I figured she would need to know. She was going to meet him sooner than later. I just hoped she wouldn't get mad.

"About that guy I like," I said. I needed to tell her.

"Lady Hepa and daughter, could you please join us?" a servant said, bowing to us from the doorway.

"Yes, honey?" my mother ignored the servant.

"Never mind," I added. It wasn't the time to tell her.

My mother stood and pulled me up with her. She took my hand, and we left together. The servant led us back into the open courtyard. It was strange to see it lit by lamps as the sun was setting. Yes, Seth would be beyond worried. The courtyard was empty, except for one last lady that was standing near the columns.

Lady Saska smiled as we approached. That wasn't a good sign.

"My husband agreed with me that we should probably use you as an alliance with the Assyrians. They have several royal families looking for wives. Lord Enil just lost his fourth wife in childbirth. I think you would make a great wife for him," Lady Saska taunted us. I had no idea who she was talking about, but the suggestion did seem to anger my mother.

"We might even be able to get you together with him tonight," Lady Saska added. "He does like to try out his wives before bringing them back with him."

My mother glared at Lady Saska. The princess was just trying to upset my mother, and it was working. But I still didn't understand; why was she determined to throw me to random men? Was she that set on hurting my mother? Or did she have something against me? Maybe it was women in general that threatened her. Lady Saska was just one of those plain old mean people. She smiled at my mother's anger. She had to have something against my mother. I was just a pawn to get her upset.

I tugged on my mother's hand as our guides continued to walk through the courtyard. My mom followed behind me as I followed the servant.

"We are not going anywhere with any men tonight," I told my mother. Her anger calmed a little. "She's just playing you."

"I know, sweetie. I know. It's just that this is what I wanted to protect you from," my mom told me.

"And it's what I'm going to protect you from now," I added, squeezing her hand.

My mom smiled. "You grew up too fast. You do know that."

"Not grown up enough that I still don't need my mom," I replied as we turned another corner. "Don't leave me."

My mother smiled and squeezed my hand back.

"Never, honey, never," she said as we arrived at our destination.

We were led back to the same ornately decorated room from earlier. We stopped behind our guides and waited while the music stopped, and Prince Saru said something. Then we were allowed to enter. I felt like an animal on display as all eyes turned to us. Many men in the room stared greedily at me. I hated being paraded around like that, but I kept my chin up and walked behind my mother. There were only two empty seats, which were really just pillows on the floor; it was no question where we were to be seated. I looked around at all the faces watching us. We were truly the center of attention and I was out of my element. I counted it as life lesson number thirty-nine: dealing with strangers in a strange land. It was something I'd have to get used to. Let the games begin.

CHAPTER 10

ESCAPING THE PAST

The dinner was more elaborate than I expected, and much more casual. People were all seated when we arrived. But it wasn't until after Lady Saska arrived that the meal was served, and no one sat still. People milled about from table to table, and everyone talked to everyone while meals were be served and eaten. We had to have been seated at the most popular table as every man between twenty and fifty stopped by to introduce themselves. It was because my mother's cousin had informed all who were present that I was to be married off. Each man thought I had a choice in the matter and tried to impress me.

The men were all a variety in age, coloring, and dress. There was the old guy that brought his grown sons with him. His sons would have been a more suitable age match, but I had the distinct feeling that he was the one looking for a wife. Another man stopped by who was as wide as he was tall. Yet another was barely a teen, and his mother introduced him to me. That would make a really good match, considering he probably hadn't even hit puberty yet... I would have laughed at the display if I didn't know how close my life could have been to that. My mother found no humor in it, and reservedly greeted each person.

Her own future husband wasn't around. It seemed the king was too busy to come himself. He had ordered one of his sons to come in his place to collect my mother. He son was cordial, but I could see him sneaking glances at Lady Saska. I had no doubts about who had planned where my mother would be going. I kind of wondered if my mother would actually make it there or not. The evil soon-to-be queen appeared more than thrilled each time she looked at my mother sitting next to the king's son.

It wasn't until halfway through the meal that a tingle shot down my arm. Seth had arrived. I hadn't thought that he'd be invited, but he was the ambassador from Egypt for the time being, even if he refused to stay in the palace. Seth arrived dressed in his Egyptian military garb, yet somehow he seemed more regal than most of the men in the room. Maybe it was because he wasn't afraid to be half naked in front of a room full of ogling women, and yes, they were all ogling my boyfriend, or maybe it was just the way he held himself. Seth was born for the role he was playing. The prince greeted him like all the other guests, even though it was only days before that he denied Seth my mother to take back to Egypt.

Seth entered the feast and sat where room was made for him, between two women. He watched me from across the room as Dee stood behind him. I tried not to stare back. I couldn't give away that I knew him since that would put him in danger. He talked with the men and women at his table and carried on like he had attended many of these meals. I watched as people around him laughed at his story. I was jealous. Seth was mine. When he stood and walked around the room, it was obvious he knew several of the people present.

"The young Egyptian is one to look at," my mother commented to me quietly.

I looked back down at my mostly full plate when Seth

caught my stare again. He only smirked. He was fine playing the playboy of the room. I got the feeling that the man I met back in my time was actually pretty close to his normal personality in his own time. The women around him were all fawning over him. I had to stop looking. It was making me upset.

"I guess," I replied, stabbing whatever meat it was in the bowl in front of me.

"I think he's even a bit more handsome than his father," my mother added, laughing at my response at being caught looking at Seth.

"You knew his father?" I asked, thankful to be able to turn my attention to her and not Seth being drooled over by the women.

"Everyone knows his father," my mother replied. "General Paramessu is one of the best military leaders to come to Egypt in centuries. Any king out there has tried to bribe the general at one point to join their side. Everyone wants a piece of that man. He is good at what he does. They say his son will follow in his footsteps, and by what I've seen the past few months, I have no doubt the young man will be even better than his father."

There was something behind my mother's explanation. She knew too much about General Paramessu that I suspected that my father must have been more than just another soldier. I really wanted to know what she was hiding, but it wasn't the place to try to get more out of her. All around us people were casually chatting, but they were no doubt listening to us talk. We were caught in a game at the palace. No one could really say what they thought, and no one could do what they really wanted to do. This wasn't a time I wanted to be a part of, but somehow I was strangely connected to it. My mother smiled as another man came over and sat beside her, introducing himself. The line of possible suitors had not dwindled yet.

When our table was finally free of guests, Seth made a beeline for us. I tried not to acknowledge him, as all eyes were upon me, but I failed miserably. Hopefully they would all think it was just a little crush like the rest of the women in the room seemed to have on him, even if it wasn't the truth. In reality, I needed to tell Seth it would be fine, the lines were fully recharged. I needed to tell him I was sorry for running off without him, but all I received was an angry stare. I was beginning to wonder if Logan did stop by and talk with Seth and Dee.

"Lady Hepa, let me be one among many to congratulate you on your upcoming marriage," Seth spoke to my mother, completely ignoring me now that he was closer. Even when he was angry he looked good. I knew why every woman in the room was drooling over him. "As congratulations, my father has authorized me to lend you Nadim, a faithful servant."

Dee was standing behind Seth with his head bowed. I kept my mouth from dropping at Seth's words. Dee wasn't a servant. He was a free man back in Egypt, and came from a prestigious family. What game were the guys playing now? Could his charioteer even be lent out as a servant? That didn't seem reasonable to me, and they never discussed this as a plan in my presence.

"Travel between countries can be wrought with danger. We vowed that when we found you that we would protect you. Please accept my gift," Seth bowed his head to my mother. "He is well trained to protect you, and will ensure that you arrive in Anatolia unharmed."

"Oh, I can't," my mother began, but I stopped her. If Seth was lending out Dee, it was for a reason.

"Mother, you must think of your safety. He looks like an able warrior to protect you," I added. I couldn't give away who they were to me, but I had to get my mother to agree.

"That won't be necessary," Prince Saru said as he

joined our table. I didn't even see him approach. "Thank you for the offer, General Seti, but we can aptly protect her."

"Didn't she get hurt the last time she was promised to someone, before she ever even left the palace here?" I asked.

My mother grabbed my hand and tried to cover my mouth. It was out of place for me to be talking, and she hoped that I wouldn't get in trouble. They didn't have much tolerance around here for differing opinions. I only knew the tale second hand, and I would have said more, but I said enough for Prince Saru to pause. He couldn't deny that detail.

"That's why we hope she will accept our gift," Seth added. "When we found her alone in the desert, we promised her safety. We are only trying to keep our promise."

Prince Saru assessed Seth for his honesty before nodding and walking away. At least that battle seemed to be won. I wanted to know more of their plan, but kept my mouth shut. I was sure once alone, Dee would tell us.

"Would you please join us for a little bit of our meal?" my mother asked Seth and Dee.

"I regretfully must decline," Seth replied graciously. "We are heading back to Egypt as soon as we can. I must go back and be with my men, and make sure everything is ready."

My mother stood and walked a ways with Seth as he was leaving. I could only hear her thank Seth's father for bringing her home, and then Seth was gone. My heart broke as he walked out of my view. He didn't even look back at me once. I tried to hide my disappointment. I had really pissed him off. That wasn't my intention, and something was lost along the way. More than likely it was Logan, but since he was still helping me, I couldn't yell at him yet. My mother returned to our table and sat beside me.

"He told me to tell you that there was once a woman he loved more than life itself. He trusted her to do the right thing, and he was never disappointed in her. He just wished she would let him in on her plans so that he didn't have to worry all the time about her," my mother told me. I was unsure if she knew Seth was speaking to me or not. "That is sound marriage advice." She winked. Yes, she knew what he meant.

I went back to looking only at my meal. It was the best way to ignore all the stares. The men in the room were eyeing me over for marriage, and the women were giving me hate stares like I had personally made Seth leave the party. I felt like an animal on display, and it wasn't fun. Anyone comfortable walking into a college party and being the center of attention, well, anyone but me, would feel as awkward as I did now. Half these men were old enough to be my father, and several even brought their wives with. I wasn't enjoying the dinner in the least, but there was nothing I could do at the moment. I couldn't wait to get away from it all. My chalcedony were recharged, but I couldn't just disappear from the dinner.

My mother took all the stares in stride. It didn't even seem to register to her that we were the center of attention. I wish I could be as strong, or maybe as ignorant as her, but I could not. The longer we sat, the more I wanted to go home. This world wasn't where I wanted to be, at least not without Seth. He made everything all better, and the past more tolerable.

I felt all alone at the party with Seth gone, but the tingles in my arm let me know he hadn't actually left the palace. He was still around. I didn't know where, but I knew. Dee stood behind my mother and watched over her like a dutiful soldier. He didn't give away that Seth was around, though he had to know. As the meal progressed and people continued to mingle, Seth was watching and waiting, and it made all the difference. I didn't feel quite as alone any more. I didn't know if Logan had told him his plan, but I was sure he was waiting for me now. No matter how mad he was, he still cared.

I needed to find time to talk to him, but I had to sit through the dinner first. I was obligated to play the part of a girl waiting to be married off. Looking around the crowded room, I saw that many people were dressed like my mother and I, but quite a few others were not. They had to be from different countries, yet I didn't know enough to know who was who. In reality, the only ones I could pick out were the Egyptians as Dee, in his half-dressed garb, gave it away easily. As I looked from face to face of all these different people, I could tell that not all of them were friendly. Seth might have been completely correct to leave Dee behind. I wasn't sure of the safety of even the party right now. Prince Saru didn't seem to care or mind, but I saw it in the eyes of many there. Not everyone at this party was friends.

When Prince Saru had declared the feast a success, music and entertainment came out. Costume-clad women danced as men drank more. Many of the men were close to being, or already were, drunk. It was worse than a frat party. At least there the guys were young and stupid. These were all grown men who would sorely regret their night the next day. My mother noticed the rowdiness increasing, and she nodded to me to stand. I followed her as she led me to the doorway. We were not the only women calling it quits for the night. In fact, most of them were excusing themselves from their tables. I didn't blame any of them. I wasn't sure I would have wanted to stay around the crowd, and was glad my mother was leading me away. Before we could leave, Lady Saska blocked our exit route.

"Lady Hepa," Lady Saska said with a little drawl to her voice, her words a little slurred. She had obviously had too much to drink. "Prince Saru would like to speak to you."

Lady Saska pointed across the dinner hall to her visibly drunk husband. I highly doubted he wanted to speak to anyone, but I had to keep my mouth shut. I had already got enough stares tonight from my mother for not talking properly. My mother looked to me briefly, and then to the Prince. She nodded to Lady Saska and walked quickly back through the crowd. Dee hesitated on what to do.

"Little Egyptian soldier," Lady Saska said to Dee. There was nothing little about Dee. He may be thin, but he stood almost a head taller than the other men in the room. "You better follow her close. You never know when she might need protecting."

I discreetly nodded to Dee, and he turned and followed my mother. He wasn't sent just to protect my mother, and as my friend he was worried about me. As soon as they were both far enough away, Lady Saska waved a man over to stand beside her.

"Lord Enil has just been dying to spend some time with you to get to know you," Lady Saska explained with a giddy happiness in her eyes. A short, pudgy man that looked twice as old as my mother was standing next to Lady Saska, ruddy-faced.

"My beautiful little princess," the man said, he grabbed my hand and kissed it—or more like licked it.

I pulled my hand back, and he laughed. He was disgusting with bits of food still stuck in his beard, and he was old and smelly. I didn't plan to stand around being licked by some drunk man, no matter who he was.

"She is a shy one," the man said to Lady Saska. I wasn't shy. I just knew enough that the man had more intentions than just kissing my hand. "I like them that way. Much more fun in bed."

I cringed at his brashness. He had to be crazy, too. There was no way I was going to any bed with that man.

"He would like to walk you back to the women's wing,"

Lady Saska explained. She leaned in closer to me and added. "He is important. He gets whatever he wants. Make sure you don't offend him or disappoint him, if you get what I mean. We need his trade to continue protecting the city and to guarantee protection of your mother on her way north. If you fail to do just as he pleases, that Egyptian soldier won't be enough to guard her. "

My mouth fell open at her boldness and insinuation of what would happen if I didn't sleep with the drunken old guy next to her. She pushed my mouth shut with the tip of her decorated fingers and grinned. She was doing just as she wanted from the beginning. Lady Saska was truly a wicked woman.

"I have been trying to get to your mother since the day she returned. She had always acted like she's better than the rest of us. Well guess what? She's not. When she finds you sleeping with this man it will finally break her. Please enjoy his company. I hear he likes it really rough," Lady Saska added. She smiled evilly and pushed the old man my way.

Lord Enil snaked his arm around my waist and grabbed my butt as he pushed me forward and out of the room. Seth had to be nearby, and I hoped that he was close. I knew how Seth would react. Outside the room the old man, who was stronger than I expected, pushed me back against one of the pillars that lined the corridor. Using his weight, he pressed his old flabby body into me. People passed by going into and out of the dining hall. No one stopped him.

"Such a pretty little toy," the man said, his breath was hot on my face and stunk of booze.

Lord Enil moved in to kiss me, and I couldn't help but react. My knee flew up between his legs, and he dropped to the ground howling. I backed away as people started to come over to see what was wrong with him. My mother and Dee exited the dining hall at that exact moment, and

Dee didn't even look twice at the man on the floor.

"This way," Dee directed me as he pulled my mother from the scene.

"No," my mother said as she chose a different direction. "We can't go that way. They will expect Mari to head back to the women's quarters to hide. All the women are like that. They never expect us to have brains."

I followed behind as my mother led. We were getting further away from Seth. The palace was a maze of hallways to me, but my mother knew what she was doing. She led us through halls and courtyards as we avoided all people and wove our way between dangers. She picked a route that wasn't direct, and I was getting confused to where we were. Nevertheless, we stayed hidden and safe. When we finally stopped, she looked to me.

"Are you all right?" she asked, pulling me into the moonlight in the small, unfurnished room.

"Yes, Mom," I replied with an eye roll. "I can take care of myself."

My mother pulled me to the corner of the room and made me sit down.

"Go get Paramessu's son," my mother told Dee. Even my mother knew Seth had stayed around. That worried me a bit. How many others knew he was around also?

"Is it safe to stay here for a little bit?" Dee asked my mother. She nodded. "I'll go get Seti and return here with him. Don't go far, but if you do, we will find you." My mother nodded.

Dee disappeared into a dark hallway, and we huddled down in our hiding spot. Their agreement to keep her safe was more than either my mother or Seth told me. It wasn't optimal to be running off in the night, but we would be fine once the boys were both back. Logan would come and help us, and we could go home. We were almost there, and we needed to leave soon.

"Mari?" my mother asked as darkness surrounded us and we waited for Dee and Seth to return.

"Yes Mom?" I replied.

"You love Paramessu's son, don't you," she asked.

Gosh, I hope I wasn't that obvious.

I was glad it was dark, and she couldn't see me blush. I had just told him that a day ago. It was kind of strange to be talking to anyone, especially my mother, about it. We were hiding out to save my life, and she was wondering about my love life. That was my mother; she always did have strange priorities.

"Why would you say that?" I replied.

"I saw how you looked at him, and he at you," my mom answered. "Most of the people in that room would have never noticed, but I've been in love before. I know what it looks like."

"Yes, Mom. I love Seth," I replied, wondering why we were even having this conversation, but glad to be able to tell her.

"It's strange how love can work. You've only just come here. By the way, I thought you came with Sangre's son," my mom answered. Yes, she needed to get all the details while we hid out.

"I came with Logan, but I love Seth," I replied.

"How can that be?" she asked, looking for more information from me.

"I met him at college months ago. He was the football quarterback. Yes, the one who saved me in the fall from those guys that were attacking college girls. I tutored him and his *brothers*, Dee and Ty. They were all from the past," I explained, giving her the shortened version of everything. "He was the reason I went back into the past at Thanksgiving. I went back to find him."

"Now that makes more sense. I couldn't for the life of me figure out why you went back. I thought maybe it was an accident or that you were looking for your father." My mom put her arm around me.

"Nope, not an accident," I replied. "The goddess took Seth and his brothers back to the past. I didn't want to be without them, and didn't think before just going off to be with him."

"Love is always like that. You never imagine doing certain things, but you will for love. You know it's going to be complicated," she added.

"I know, Mom. I'm sitting in the past, hiding out to get back to the future with my family. It's all really complicated," I replied, and we both laughed. "This whole world is complicated."

"And that's why you have to listen to me. Mari, you need to get out of here. I don't know what they will do to you, and I can't protect you. I'm as good as gone. Even if we stay, they are sending me away in the morning. And it would be my word against Lady Saska's. Lord Enil is a powerful man. Prince Saru knows that, and will want to make him happy..." my mom started.

"I didn't mean to, Mom. It was just an automatic reaction. Lady Saska basically told him he could have his way with me, and I was to obey. I just couldn't do that. When he tried to kiss me, I just reacted," I interrupted her quickly. "I'm sorry. I wasn't trying to complicate things for you."

"And I'm glad about that. I raised you to be as strong as your father. But that doesn't work here in this world. Women are tools in this country. We are not people. I can't have you stay here, you need to go home." My mom hugged me like it was a last goodbye.

"I'm not leaving you here. They plan to send you north and marry you off. You deserve to go find Dad," I replied. "You can't do that if you're bartered off. Let me take you home and from there we can make plans to find dad. If you guys loved each other like Seth and I do, I know he will remember you and will be thinking of you. I'm learning how to control this time travel stuff. I know we can get you to him. You can be with him and be happy."

My mom hugged me. "You grew up too fast. I'm here trying to protect you, and all you want to do is protect me. When did that happen? You used to be my little girl, and now you're running around saving me and falling in love. When did I get so old?"

"You're not old, Mom. I'll take you back to Dad. You can be happy," I answered.

I was convincing her to travel back with me. I wasn't even trying that at this point, but I could feel that I was swaying her over with my words. I truly wanted to find my dad and get to know him. It was a piece of my life that had always been missing.

"You'd really do that?" she asked.

"Yes, Mom. I'd do anything for you, and I have always kind of wanted to meet my dad." I hugged her back tightly.

Time had passed as we talked, and I was unsure how long we had been sitting there. It was cool in the room, but together we stayed warm. We were sitting in the dark whispering for quite some time, yet still no one came by. Either the palace had to be huge, or they weren't looking for us. It was strange to not hear another sound. It was completely quiet.

"I always wanted you to meet him, too," she replied.

"Let me send you home in the future," I replied. I needed her back there safe from this time.

"Right now?" she asked.

"Yes right now. I can't have them find you with me, if they do come. I can leave at any time, but you can only leave if you're with me. I promise to not be far behind. I'll wait a little longer for Seth and Dee, and then call for

Logan. I'll get everyone home, and then we'll decide what to do next. I'm sure Seth and Dee will know who my father is, and how we can find him. Together we'll face the future and the past," I explained. My mother nodded. "Please, let me save you first, and we'll all come home right behind you."

"Sounds like a plan. You are very much like him, even though I raised you. Your father always had the plans, and now you do. I will do as you ask, as long as you promise to come right home after getting the boys back. They will be in danger if you leave them here. They'll be the first targets of Prince Saru. He always suspected the Egyptians of taking me to begin with, but he could never prove it since there was no trace of me left," she replied. I figured that much. They would think Dee and Seth took my mother again, and she would be gone and unable to prove that they did not.

"Logan," I called into the darkness. I waited a few seconds without him instantly appearing before realizing he wasn't coming.

I turned to my mother. I had no time to wait for Logan to come this time around. I could send her home without him, and when he came he could take both of the guys. My arm warmed, and I thought of the future. Ty and I had worked out a technique where I could push the person into the future and not go with them. I'd do that now, and then wait for the guys to come back. I had no time to think about it. I needed my mother safe.

I placed my warm hand on her and saw time speed up. I found our home where Ty was waiting.

"I'm sending you back to my room where Ty is. We should get back soon after you. I'll see you in moments," I told her. She smiled at me.

"It really is great seeing you grow up," she told me as the tingle began to engulf her body. She leaned down and kissed my forehead. "Your father is General Meryamun;

he is General Paramessu's partner, running the Egyptian military."

His name gave me tingles. *My father had a name.* He was becoming more real each moment. My mother was a great parent, but she couldn't make up for him not being there. She couldn't hide her sadness that he didn't get to see me grow up also. I never considered going back to find him, but was excited now by the prospect. I was going to get to meet my father. It was exciting and scary at the same time. The man who risked everything to get me safe had been an illusion my whole life, and now he was becoming real.

She faded from me, and I was left alone, lost in a palace in a time I didn't belong. Logan didn't show up, but I kind of expected that. He wasn't the most reliable. I wouldn't have to wait long, but I was truly alone for the first time since I got into the past. I had to believe Seth would come to me. Otherwise, I was screwed.

I felt the tingles before I heard the footsteps of Seth and Dee's approach. They were coming my direction fast. There must not have been anyone around for them to take such a direct route to me.

"Logan," I called into the darkness for the tenth time. I had no idea why Logan wasn't replying. It wasn't a travel-free zone like Ty's room, since I had just sent my mother back, but I could find no more excuses. He was starting to annoy me.

"Mari," Seth whispered into the darkness as they came closer.

"Right here," I replied as I reached up and grabbed his arm. He was passing me near the doorway into the room as he looked for me. His lips crushed against mine instantly as he pulled me to my feet.

"Where is your mother?" he asked.

"I sent her back," I replied, not getting enough air since his hug was crushing me.

"I was worried about you when we came back, and you were gone," he scolded me, but didn't let me go. "I knew what you would have done, but I was still worried. I told you not to get involved. They're not kind to women here. Did you travel into the palace?"

"No. Logan took me. He came along to help us. I told him to help me," I admitted.

"Now what's the plan?" Seth asked, not even caring.

"Logan can take one of you back at a time, and then I'll follow since I can go on my own," I replied. "Logan," I called again, a little louder. Maybe he couldn't hear me.

Logan appeared in front of us.

"Here I was thinking you forgot about us," I told him. I was being completely honest, although I had an idea that maybe he was leaving us alone on purpose.

"I came as soon as I could," Logan replied. He was dressed ornately in clothing I didn't recognize. "I have a role to play here. I couldn't just disappear from where I was." His explanation was legit enough, but I was still worried.

"Can you take Dee back first?" I asked. Seth was my main concern, but if they caught us anytime soon, Dee would take the blame for my missing mother. He was in more danger than Seth at this point and I owed him to be safe after he saved me before.

"Of course," Logan replied, taking Dee and disappearing into thin air.

Logan and Dee were gone, and I was left alone with Seth.

"Are you really okay?" he asked, moving me closer to the window in the dark room we were sitting in. Just like my mother had, he was looking me over from head to toe.

"You smell clean and don't have any outside bruising," he commented.

"I smell like when you try perfumes at a department store and instead of one scent, you come out smelling like a disgusting mixture of all of them. It isn't clean," I explained, and Seth laughed.

"You didn't get hurt at all?" he asked suspiciously. "I felt you get scared not too long ago. That's why it took Dee a while to find me. I was already running to you."

"Yes. Some old guy tried to kiss me, and I kind of kneed him in the crotch," I replied, shrugging. I was a bit frightened of the old man. He was way stronger than me, but I was safe now.

Seth laughed, and I had to cover his mouth to keep him quiet. He kissed the inside of my hand, and I dropped it. "That's my girl. I know I don't need to worry about you. You will protect yourself, but still, I will always worry. You're my girl, and I don't want you to get hurt."

"I don't try to, you know that," I answered.

"I know, but somehow adventure seems to always find you," Seth replied. He didn't sound happy about that.

I laid my head against him as we sat back down to wait. Logan didn't return immediately, but time traveling wasn't an exact science. You could aim to get somewhere and be off by minutes, or even hours—days in my case. I was getting better at it, but it was still hard. Logan had even admitted to me that he wasn't always exact.

"You wouldn't believe how crazy I felt inside the moment you were gone. I knew before we even went up to the room that you were missing. Dee had a hard time holding me back from marching into the palace and demanding you," Seth told me as he rubbed my back. "You are mine."

"Now that would have worked, right?" I teased. I could picture Seth doing just that. He would be fine if it were a princess, not a prince, running the country. Any woman would give him exactly what he wanted, but I had a feeling Prince Saru would never give Seth what he asked for.

"I wasn't exactly thinking about what might or might not work. All I knew was I needed you back," Seth replied. "I need you like I need air. Please promise me not to just leave me."

"Can you promise me the same?" I asked.

I knew the answer, and so did he. Neither one of us could promise that. We had as much control of our fate as the goddess allowed. Once I took him back to the future with me, there was no guarantee he would be allowed to stay.

"I sent Logan to tell you," I added.

He shook his head with a laugh. "No message from him. Just me being crazy by losing you."

"I'm sorry," I replied. That was never my intention.

"I know neither of us can promise to never disappear. Then promise me that no matter what time or place we end up, we will always find each other," Seth replied, drawing circles on my back as he rubbed it.

"That I can promise." I tilted my head up and kissed him. I'd never stop fighting to be beside him, and he was now promising me the same. I didn't even have to doubt Seth or his love. Our fates were already intertwined.

"What was it like?" Seth asked curiously. I pulled my head up to question him before he added, "Your short stint as royalty."

I smacked his arm. "This isn't royalty. This is being caught in a game I never learned how to play. They are all evil here. I don't know if I'd even be close to the same person I am now if I was raised here. I'm thankful my mother took me to the future to raise me."

"Then it wasn't all sitting around drinking exotic drinks and eating the most expensive foods while frolicking about?" I could practically hear a grin in Seth's voice.

"Nothing close. Let's just say that I get the very

distinct feeling that the attempt on my mother's life that she lived through came from right within the palace. These people are evil, and the women might just be at the heart of it." I cuddled into his warm arms. "I can't wait to get out of here."

"You missed me then?" Seth asked, all seriousness in his voice.

"Of course I missed you. I was worried about what you would do, and I will have to thank Dee for being the voice of reason. I tried to tell you my plans to get my mother, but you didn't listen. I thought Logan would tell you," I replied.

Seth pulled off his ceremonial headdress and scratched at his short hair.

"I can't help wanting to protect you. I'll probably feel that way forever," Seth replied. I snuggled in close.

"I love that about you," I replied. I truly did. Maybe I should have planned more to save my mother, but I knew that if anything went wrong, Seth would be there with me. I had faith that he would save me.

"I just want you to remember I can be included in all of this, too," I added. I needed him to see me as an asset. The whole time they planned, I was never included. It was my mother, after all, and I was the one with the time travel ability.

Seth kissed my forehead. "I promise to include you. I tend to forget you're not like other girls."

"Got that right," I replied. "And you've never been like all the other guys in my book."

Seth laughed and hugged me tight.

"Marcella. I don't know how this is possible. You run off without telling me. Drag me into some political war. Run away and hide in a palace where we can be found any moment. And somehow this all makes me love you more. I'm not going to let them have you to marry off to Prince Arik-ninari."

"Who's that?" I asked.

"Not the one trying to kiss you?" Seth asked, confused.

"No. I'm sure that was Lord Enil," I replied. I hadn't heard of a Prince Arik-ninari, and the name didn't ring a bell as anyone I was introduced to at the dinner. This was someone completely new and that was confusing.

"What?" Seth asked, anger starting to rise. "Your mother left you alone with Lord Enil?" The name alone was upsetting him.

"Not exactly. Lady Saska sent my mother to talk to the prince, and then hauled me off to give me to Lord Enil," I explained, lacing my fingers in his and keeping him from standing up. I didn't understand why he was angry.

"On purpose?" Seth asked.

"Um, yes. She told me to do anything I needed to do to please him since he was important to trade," I replied. The guy was a creep, but it seemed his reputation preceded him. "Too bad I have trouble following orders."

"I can't believe her. I knew that woman was trouble, but Lord Enil? She must really dislike you," Seth told me as he pulled me back into his arms. His heart was still beating fast.

"I think she really dislikes my mother. Who is this other one trying for me?" I asked. I was sure I didn't meet the other prince.

"I have only ever heard the name. I've never met him before. He's an Assyrian prince. Prince Saru wants to get in close with Assyria for protection," Seth explained.

"Doesn't he want in close with everyone?" That seemed like more likely to me.

"Everyone except Egypt." Seth chuckled like it was a funny thing to do.

"Why not Egypt, too?" I asked.

"Prince Saru thinks that by having both Assyria and Hittite as allies, he can fight against Egypt. Nothing he does will stand up to my dad if my dad wants to march this way. Hittite and Assyria aren't going to support Nahrin completely. They might send some troops, but nothing that will matter. They just see it as a buffer zone to keep their own countries safe. Saru can't see that, and is dumb for thinking his alliance will keep him on the throne. There was only one reason his father was doing well, and that was because he was controlling the Nahrin and keeping it safe. He sided with no one, and fought with no one. Prince Saru isn't that wise," Seth explained.

I snuggled in close under his arm and against his chest. He was warm, and the beat of his heart was back to normal. Our wait was getting longer, yet no one was finding us. We continued to sit, hiding. It had been a long day, and I couldn't help my eyes drooping. Maybe I was tired, or maybe I was just content. I was safe in Seth arms. He stroked my head as I laid there.

"The goddess was right. I was meant to find you. Even if I lived a thousand lifetimes, it was always supposed to be you," Seth told me. It was strange to hear him put words to what I felt.

I sat up a little and looked around. Seth noticed.

"What is it?" he asked, on alert.

"Nothing. I thought I heard something," I replied. "Logan's never taken this long. I really should send you back, and I can stay here alone to get my power back."

"You can't come with me?" he asked.

"No, I have two stones, but I already used one on my mother," I explained. I didn't regret sending my mother back. "I can still send you back, but it will be a couple days before I can leave." I could see in the dim light that he was scowling. I guess a couple days wasn't good enough for him. "Seth, if you get caught with me, I won't be able to save you if they take you. I'll do anything to protect you."

"As will I for you. The next time you return here there will be no waiting around doing something else. I'm going to marry you, and then no more men in this time can claim you. You are mine and mine alone," he declared, sending shivers down to my toes. I liked the sound of that. I was already his from the first time he kissed me, but I was never going to admit that.

"I just don't know where Logan is," I replied. "He should be here by now. He's better at the time travel thing than I am."

"Maybe he's not coming. Could he have a reason not to come?" Seth asked. I had told Seth everything that happened, but maybe not clearly enough.

"I was afraid he wouldn't come for you. I never told him that I had two stones just so that I'd be able to get you back home with me," I admitted. Even now that I knew the real reasons behind his leaving me all the time, it didn't change anything. I might never be able to trust Logan.

"You thought this might happen?" Seth asked. He wasn't mad or accusing, just stating a fact, analyzing the situation.

"He told me that he still cared about me, and I blew him off. He said he'd do anything to be my friend, even help save you because it made me happy, but there was just something about him. I thought I could trust him, and thought the old Logan was still in him, but I'm not sure the old Logan was anyone that still exists," I replied. "I'm getting a feeling that the new Logan doesn't plan to come back for you at all."

"Old Logan?" Seth questioned.

"I told you that I dated him for two years in high school. Back then he was different. The look in his eyes was different. He was kind and caring, but now? I don't know. I never saw him doing anything different since he's been back in my life, but Ty had stories. He said you guys saw a lot of changes in him after I broke up with him," I answered.

"You're the girl?" Seth stated it as a question. I had no

idea what he was asking.

"The girl?" I questioned back.

"He tried to ask you out for months, but never had the nerve to. He figured you'd turn him down, but eventually he asked you and you said yes," Seth added. That didn't sound like Logan. He could have asked any girl in my high school, ones with or without boyfriends, and all would have said yes to him.

"I wasn't the girl no matter what *the girl* means," I replied.

"The girl he said was the one. You know. The one person you find that will make you see the world in colors, and without them your world is dull," Seth replied.

"Wait a second," I added. "It was never like that with us. I mean, yeah we dated. I kissed him, but never went as far as I did with you. It wasn't like that between us. It was more like puppy love. We would look at each other and sigh kind of love. It wasn't real like this is." I tapped his chest. He needed to know there was a difference. No one would ever compare to Seth. What I had with Seth was much more than I ever anticipated. "What we have is real. What I had with him was first love, puppy dog love," I explained. Seth had to know the difference. "I've never felt this way with anyone before, and I doubt I ever will with anyone else. Logan has to know that. I love you and only you."

Seth pulled me to his chest and nuzzled into my head. I guess I said the right things.

"I know what we have is different. This is what Logan thought he had with you. I feel kind of bad for the guy, because what you describe with him is nothing close to what I feel for you. But he thinks it's this anyways. I have a good feeling he isn't coming for me," Seth added. It was exactly what I was thinking.

"Probably not," I replied.

Seth held me tight and shared his warmth with me. I

was safe in the crazy world of the past. Now I just needed to keep it that way.

"What do we do now?" I asked. I had seen from the window that we could make our way out of the palace if we wanted. There was a direct line from the window to the wall, and the wall wasn't even solid here. I wasn't sure what was right outside, but it was worth a risk. I had no doubt my mother led us this way to escape. It might have been her original escape route she used years ago.

Seth looked at the window, too. He must have seen the way also.

"We wait here," he said. "And hope your powers recover from sending your mother home sooner than they find us."

"Why don't we run?" I asked. I was curious that he didn't deem that an option.

"Because they will be looking for you in the city," Seth replied. "Your mother escaped the city while they searched the palace for her. They never expected she would leave the palace. I doubt they will be as careless this time. They will be looking around the city first this time. We might be able to go unnoticed here long enough for the stones to recover. It's safer to sit and wait."

"Might?" I asked. I didn't like the sound of that.

Seth shrugged. "I don't know. I just know that I'm not leaving your side, and I'm not putting us into further danger. Sitting here is the best option for now."

"And I won't let you die for me," I replied stubbornly. He wasn't going to win that fight. I just had to survive two more days, and the chrysoprase would be rejuvenated. I could send him home any time with the carnelian that still laced my arm.

Seth hugged me tight. "How about this. We sit here and wait. If anyone finds us, you can send me back, but until then we sit together. If we stay long enough, your stone will be recovered, and we can both go home," he suggested.

That was an option I could live with. It didn't seem like anyone was looking for us for now. I could hope they wouldn't even come to this section of the palace. I nodded and leaned back against this chest. He stroked my head, and I again felt the sleepiness come over me.

"I can't believe you're the one that Logan pined over. We avoided him after you broke up with him. He was always in a terrible mood. I even remember his father calling him during one of our dinners, he yelled at him right in front of us. Every guy that ever asked you out was given a one way ticket to another time, courtesy of Logan. He was scarily powerful, yet his father had more power, and could keep him in line. You're right, Logan changed, and it wasn't for the better," Seth told me as he stroked my head. My sleepy mind was listening, but it seemed unreal. It seemed like the sweet Logan that I thought I knew didn't ever exist.

"I don't know what Logan thought we had, but I do know he was delusional. I could never compare what I feel with you to what I felt with him. This is true love." I kissed his chest as he held me tight.

"Sleep, love," Seth told me gently. "I'll stay awake and tell you if anyone comes."

"Promise?" I asked. It wasn't unlike Seth to be a martyr. I had to be sure he would actually tell me.

"Yes, I promise," Seth replied. "You can save me if you promise to get back to me as soon as you can. I need to give you more credit for what you can do. I trust that you will come to me."

"Always," I replied, closing my eyes.

Light was streaming into the window by the time I woke.

Seth was still sitting against the wall as my pillow and his eyes were half cracked open when I sat up and stretched. I was a little stiff from lying on the floor all night, but I was rested.

"No one came?" I asked, stretching my arms a second time, and trying to crack the kink in my back.

"Nope, not even a sentry around the wall. They must still be searching the city," Seth replied, sitting up now that I wasn't sleeping on him.

I looked down at my arm. The red carnelian lines snaked up my arm as normal, but the green was only around my wrist. It wasn't anywhere close to being recovered, but it was better than being completely gone. Seth took my arm as I looked at it, examining it himself.

"How long did the lines take to come back when you came here?" he asked.

"I don't exactly know," I replied as a blush started to creep into my cheeks. "I was a little distracted," I admitted while turning away. Seth chuckled and pulled my face back to him. He kissed me and then asked.

"Distracted by what?" he asked innocently, teasing me. I pushed him and stood up.

I walked over to the high-cut window and stood on my toes to peer out. No one was outside, and I had no clue where we were in the palace. The room we were sitting in was just as sparse as I thought it was when we came in the night before. It would have been nice to have a tour of the palace before my mother left, but there was nothing I could do now. We would sit and wait for the power of the stone to come back. I moved back beside Seth and sat down.

"I think it is your turn to sleep," I told him, touching the dark lines under his eyes. He looked like he hadn't slept well in weeks. Maybe he hadn't.

Seth smiled and nodded. He was running on close to nothing.

"I make a pretty nice pillow." I patted my lap, and he smiled. I was sitting against the wall and he leaned back onto my lap. He stared up at me and smiled. His dark brown eyes were happy even though they revealed his exhaustion.

"You know, this is the way I first met you," I replied, gently rubbing his head.

Seth grinned. "Oh, I remember that day. I found you and sat beside you at that tree. You didn't even notice me. I thought I'd be all smooth and sit down beside you. I'd give one of those lines I used hundreds of times, and you'd agree to go out with me. When you didn't look up from your book, I didn't know what to do. I never had a woman ignore me before. I just sat there and waited for you to be done with your book. Next thing I remember was waking up on the ground and you were gone."

I giggled. "Well, you kind of fell asleep next to me and landed in my lap."

"I did?" Seth asked in disbelief. He had no memory of the incident.

"Yeah. I wasn't sure what to do. I sat there waiting for you to wake. You didn't, and I freaked out, so I slipped out from beneath you and ran away," I admitted. Seth laughed.

"That I can imagine," Seth replied. "I did wonder for quite some time how I ended up on the ground where you had been sitting."

"Glad you didn't think I wasn't worth the hassle with my bookworm ways," I replied. I was happy he chased me down.

"I couldn't. You captured my heart the first time I saw you. I just didn't know it then," Seth answered, closing his eyes.

"You had more hair then," I commented as I rubbed the short hair he had now.

"And you were certain to stay away from me," Seth

replied. "A lot of good that did you."

I smiled and bent down to kiss him. "I'm glad you didn't give up."

"Never." Seth smiled and closed his eyes as I sat back up. "I will never give up on you."

I stroked Seth's face as he drifted off to sleep. His features softened as he fell deeper into sleep. This was my Seth, with his short, dark reddish-brown hair and smooth, tan skin. He was completely the Egyptian warrior he always was. Even back then, on my first day in college, he landed in my lap, shirtless. I smiled at the thought. He calmly slept on my lap. I couldn't help but to think back to the day I met him in the fall. His hair was longer, but that was about the only difference. He was still Seth. I never pictured then that I would fall madly in love with this guy. If I had, maybe I wouldn't have run away as quickly.

We sat for only a few hours that way as he got some rest. My mind wandered, thinking of the new world I was a part of. The past was too confusing, but when Seth walked into that party, I knew that this was where he belonged. He was a beacon of light in the strange world of the past, but by the way others looked at him, they thought he was the light to a new way. He was special, not just to me, but to everyone. I could take him with me to the future, but we would need to come back. He was meant to be in this world. I could see what the goddess meant. No matter how long I stole him for myself, he would eventually need to return and live out what fate had planned for him here. I just hoped it would be safe enough, and I could go with him. I wanted a role in this past beside him. I didn't ever want to be without him again. He made me feel real; he made me see the world in more colors than I could imagine.

When he sat up and rubbed his eyes, I noticed my feet were completely asleep. I had no clue how long he had napped. The lines had grown a little on my arm.

"Any noise?" he asked, looking around.

"Nope. Nothing," I replied. The wing of the palace we were in was eerily quiet.

"Good," Seth replied. He stood and stretched his body. It couldn't be comfortable sleeping on the floor like he had. At least I had more of him to use as a pillow and bed. He slept mainly on the floor with only my lap for a pillow. He walked to the window and looked out. It had to be close to midday. My stomach growled. Seth smiled and turned to me.

"Hey. I can't help it," I complained. "I didn't grow up in a time where you went without food for days and thought it was okay."

"How much did the chalcedony recover?" Seth asked, coming back to me and looking at my arm. It wasn't much, but the line was longer. "If you need food, I'll go find you some." Seth offered.

"No," I replied, grabbing his arm. "I can go without a meal or two." I didn't want to put him in danger.

"But not without water. When it gets dark, I will go get us water," Seth told me. I had to nod. He was correct. We would at least need water. I could give him that much.

Seth sat back down and wrapped his arms around me. Waiting for the lines to recover was horribly boring, but to have him next to me was going to pass time nicely. I would never get bored of his touch.

"I was thinking," I started. I had way too much time to think while he was sleeping. "That maybe we should come back here. Well, not here, here, but back here to the past. Like your place in the past. Something tells me you're meant to be here, and if you are, then I am, too. I'm meant to be wherever you are."

Seth squeezed me tight. "I'd like that," he agreed immediately.

"What?" I asked, pushing back from his hug. "No lecture on how the past is dangerous this time?" The first time I wanted to go to the past he was determined to stop me. I never imagined he would agree that easily. I even had part of an argument to support my idea ready.

Seth laughed. "Oh, I'd lecture you if I didn't think you had learned your lesson."

"My lesson?" I replied.

"I have no doubts you see the danger of the past now," Seth replied, pulling me close again.

"And I have no doubts you see I can handle myself," I replied, using his words. I felt the chuckle of Seth as my head was pressed to his chest.

"Yes, Mari. Ty was right. I've met my match, and can't wait to see where the world will take us." Seth kissed my forehead as I stared up at him.

"You will let me come back with you?" I asked. This was too easy. I really thought I'd have to convince him it was best for us. I was prepared to argue my side.

"Under one condition." He held up his finger to keep me from talking. "Our first trip back will be to find your father and ask his permission for us to marry. You will be my wife," Seth stated.

That was all I wanted, too. He was the future I wanted, even if we were in the past. I hugged him. I wanted nothing more than to do just that, but I never got the chance to tell him. We both heard the footsteps at the same time.

Seth stood and pulled me up with him. We swiftly moved to the next room, further away from the steps coming near. We had been found. I grasped his hand tightly. I didn't want our alone time to end. I was hoping we could sit there for days and then head home together. That wasn't going to be the case.

"You are going home now," I told him. My hand heated and time flew by. Stress made me do it faster.

"You will come back to me," Seth ordered as he felt the heat engulf him. He didn't protest or stop me. I kissed him while he was still solid.

"And we will find my father, General Meryamun, together," I replied as he faded.

I saw his mouth move and the surprise on his face. It wasn't an angry surprise, but a happy one. He melted away with that surprised smile, and I had no clue what it meant. I didn't have enough time to tell him who my father was, or ask questions, but I had a feeling Seth knew who he was. He had to. General Meryamun was his father's partner. He had to know my father.

The footsteps drew near. I would be found soon, but it didn't matter. The carnelian lines were gone, but the chrysoprase was at least a third of the way up my arm. I needed a day or two, max, to get away. I could do that, and there was enough of the line to transport me short distances if I needed to get away. I did exactly what I wanted to do. My mother, Dee, and Seth were in the future and safe. My family was safe. I had no clue where I was, but I could do this. I could survive the past because someone was waiting for me in the future. I'd never doubt what I had with Seth again. The goddess knew what she was doing when she put us together. Seth was the love of my life.

Coming in early 2015:

Aventurine (The Chalcedony Chronicles #3)

Other books by this author:
- To Stand Beside Her
- The Blue Eyes Trilogy
  - The Legend of the Blue Eyes
  - Becoming a Legend
  - Winning the Legend
- The Day Human Trilogy
  - Day Human Prince
  - Day Human King
- The Chalcedony Chronicles
  - Carnelian
  - Chrysoprase
  - Aventurine

ACKNOWLEDGMENTS

As with any work of fiction, there are many people to thank along the way.

To you, the reader. Thank you for taking the time to read this story and go on the journey with me and Mari. If you liked it, please leave a review on your favorite online bookseller (or all of them!) and connect with me. The greatest help you can do to keep a writer going is to support them by spreading the word about their books and leaving them encouraging words.

Also I would like to thank my editor and cover designers. A good editor is essential to getting the story correct. Thank you so much, Kathie, for catching all those errors. Thankfully she make this a better novel for everyone else to read. Thanks also to Ashton Brammer for the second edit to make this book even better. A thank you to Alexandria Thompson at Gothic Fate for such a pretty cover, and Lunarieen for allowing us to use your beautiful necklace. They may say *never judge a book by its cover*, but everyone does! I am grateful I was able to find great professionals to work with on this book.

I'd also like to thank my hubby for continuing to push me further down the writing road. He gives me time when I need it to work on my stories. He encourages me to keep going each and every day on this adventure. And he does all the behind-the-scenes effort to make this work. This would be so much harder without his help. So thank you, B. for pushing me off the deep end (or the cliff as I see it sometimes). And a great big thanks to my little munchkins who keep me going from before the sun comes up 'til long after it sets. Love you AK and KB.

Thank you so much for taking the time to read my novel!!

ABOUT THE AUTHOR

Originally from Wisconsin, B. Kristin currently resides in Ohio with her husband, two small children, and three cats. When not doing the mom thing of chasing kids, baking cookies, and playing outside, she is using her PhD in biology as a scientist. In her free time she is currently hard at work on multiple novels. Every day is a new writing adventure. You can find her on Twitter, Facebook, and Goodreads. She is a fan of all YA fantasy and science fiction and continues to promote good books on her own blog at www.bkristinmcmichael.com.